BORIS VIAN

Mood Indigo

Boris Vian was born at Ville d'Avray in 1920. A novelist, poet, dramatist, writer of popular songs, jazz critic, singer and trumpeter, Paris liaison for Duke Ellington and Miles Davis, friend of Jean-Paul Sartre and Raymond Queneau, and French translator of Raymond Chandler, Vian trained as an engineer and worked for a pulp and paper-making corporation until 1947. In the decade and a half before his untimely death in 1959 at the age of thirty-nine, Vian's extraordinary creative output included ten novels, four short-fiction collections, seven plays, three books of poetry, several translations, and a number of popular songs, including the antiwar anthem 'Le déserteur', which was banned by the French censors and sung by Joan Baez during the Vietnam War. Vian died from a heart attack at a screening of the film adaptation of his pulp noir novel *I Spit on Your Graves*. Half a century after his death, his most celebrated and loved novel, *L'Écume des jours* (originally published in English as *Froth on the Daydream*), has been adapted for the screen by the acclaimed director Michel Gondry, released in English under the title *Mood Indigo*.

ALSO BY BORIS VIAN

Mood Indigo

Mood Indigo

BORIS VIAN

Translated from the French by Stanley Chapman

Farrar, Straus and Giroux

New York

Farrar, Straus and Giroux
18 West 18th Street, New York 10011

Printed in the United States of America
Originally published in French in 1947 by Gallimard, Paris, as *L'Écume des Jours*
English translation originally published in 1967 by Rapp & Carroll Ltd, Great Britain, as
Froth on the Daydream
Revised English translation originally published in 1970 by Penguin Books, Great Britain
This edition originally published in 2013 by Serpent's Tail, an imprint of
Profile Books Ltd, Great Britain
This edition published in the United States in 2014 by Farrar, Straus and Giroux

Library of Congress Control Number: 2013941213
ISBN: 978-0-374-53422-6

Designed by MacGuru Ltd

Farrar, Straus and Giroux books may be purchased for educational, business,
or promotional use. For information on bulk purchases, please contact the Macmillan
Corporate and Premium Sales Department at 1-800-221-7945, extension 5442,
or write to specialmarkets@macmillan.com.

www.fsgbooks.com
www.twitter.com/fsgbooks • www.facebook.com/fsgbooks

1 3 5 7 9 10 8 6 4 2

For my Bibi

Foreword

The main thing in life is to leap to every possible conclusion on every possible occasion. For the fact is that individuals are always right – and the masses always wrong. But we should be careful not to attempt to base any rules for behaviour on this – there is no need for rules to be written down before we follow them. Only two things really matter – there's love, every kind of love, with every kind of pretty girl; and there's the music of Duke Ellington, or traditional jazz. Everything else can go, because all the rest is ugly – and the few pages which follow as an illustration of this draw their entire strength from the fact that the story is completely true since I made it up from beginning to end. Its material realization – to use the correct expression – consists basically of a projection of reality, under favourable circumstances, on to an irregularly tilting, and consequently distorting, plane of reference. Obviously it is a method, if there ever was one, that can be readily divulged.

New Orleans
10 March 1946

Mood Indigo

1

Colin finished his bath. He got out and wrapped himself in a thick woolly towel with his legs coming out at the bottom and his top coming out at the top. He took the oil from the glass shelf and sprayed its pulverized perfume on to his yellow hair. His golden comb separated the silky mop into long honeyed strands like the furrows that a happy farmer ploughs through apricot jam with his fork. Colin put back his comb and, seizing the nail-clippers, bevelled the corners of his eggshell eyelids to add a touch of mystery to his appearance. He often had to do this because they grew again so quickly. He put on the little light over the magnifying mirror and went up close to it to examine the condition of his epidermis. A few blackheads were sprouting at the sides of his nose near his nostrils. When they saw themselves in the magnifying mirror and realized how ugly they were, they immediately jumped back under the skin. Colin put out the light and sighed with relief. He took the towel from his middle and slipped a corner of it between his toes to dry away the last signs of dampness. In the glass it became perfectly clear that he was exactly like a fair-headed Jean Bellpull Rondeau in a film by Jacques Goon Luddard. His face was smooth, his ears small, his nose straight and his complexion radiant. He was always smiling, as innocently as a baby, and through having done it so often a dimple had grown into his chin. He was reasonably tall and slim-hipped; he had long legs and was very, very nice. The name Colin suited him almost ideally.

He talked to girls with charm and to boys with pleasure. He was nearly always in a good mood – and the rest of the time he slept.

He emptied his bath by boring a hole in the bottom of the tub. The light yellow ceramic clay tiles of the bathroom floor sloped in such a way that the water was orientated into an orifice situated directly above the study of the tenant in the flat below. But only a few days previously, without saying a word to Colin, the position of the study had been changed. Now the water went straight into the larder underneath.

He slipped his feet into sandals made from the skins of spotted dogfish, and put on an elegant staying-in suit – trousers of deep Atlantic-green corduroy and a jacket of walnut-brown wild taffeta. He hung the towel on the towel-rail and put the bathmat on the edge of the bath. Then he sprinkled it with rock salt to bring out any water that might still be in it. The mat was soon covered in juicy clusters of little soapy bubbles.

He came out of the bathroom and went to the kitchen to cast an eye over the last touches that were being put to the meal. Chick was coming for dinner as he did every Monday evening. He lived just round the corner. It was still only Saturday, but Colin felt he wanted to see Chick and let him sample the menu that his new cook Nicholas had been working on with such joyful serenity. Chick, a bachelor too, was the same age as Colin – twenty-two. He had the same tastes in literature – but less money. Colin's fortune was large enough for him to live in comfort without having to work for other people. But Chick had to go to see his uncle at the Ministry once a week and borrow money from him because he did not earn enough at his job as an engineer to be able to keep up with the workers he was in charge of – and it's hard to be in charge of people who are better dressed and better fed than you are. Colin helped him as much as he could and asked him round to dinner as often as he dared, but Chick's pride forced Colin to be careful and not make it obvious that he was trying to help him by doing favours too frequently.

The corridor leading to the kitchen was light because it had windows on both sides of it, and a sun shining behind each of them because Colin was fond of bright things. There were metal taps, brilliantly polished and gleaming, all over the place. The suns playing on the taps produced fairylike effects. The kitchen mice liked to dance to the sounds made by the rays of the suns as they bounced off the taps, and then run after the little bubbles that the rays burst into when they hit the ground like sprays of golden mercury. Colin stroked one of the mice as he went by. It was sleek and grey, with a miraculous sheen and long black whiskers. The cook gave them plenty to eat, but made sure that they did not get too fat. The mice kept very quiet during the day and played nowhere else but in the corridor.

Colin pushed open the gleaming kitchen door. Nicholas, the cook, was studying his control-panel. He was sitting at a no less gleaming bright yellow desk covered in dials corresponding to every piece of culinary apparatus that lined the walls. The hand for the electric cooker, set for the roast turkey, hovered between 'Almost Ready' and 'Perfectly Done'. It was nearly time to take it out. Nicholas pressed a green button which released the testing needle. It slipped in, met no resistance at all, and the hand immediately shot to 'Perfectly Done'. Nicholas clicked off the current to the cooker and switched on the plate-warmer.

'Is it going to be good?' asked Colin.

'Mr Colin can be assured that it is, sir!' confirmed Nicholas. 'The turkey is done to a turn.'

'And what have we got to start with?'

'Good Lord,' said Nicholas, 'I didn't like to create anything original so soon, sir. I've stuck to plagiarizing ffroydde.'

'You could have chosen a worse master!' remarked Colin. 'And which masterpiece from his complete works are you going to reproduce?'

'I found it on page 638 of his *Cookery and Household Management*. I'll read Mr Colin the passage in question, sir.'

Colin sat on a stool upholstered in dunlopillo and oiled silk, the same colour as the walls, as Nicholas began to read.

'First line a dish with light puff pastry. Then slice a large eel into sections about an inch thick. Place these in a saucepan and cover with white wine to which has been added a sliced onion, some chopped parsley, a sprig of thyme, a bailiff's bay leaf, a four-leaved clove-hitch of garlic and a pinch of salt and pepper . . . I couldn't pinch as much salt and pepper as I'd have liked, sir,' said Nicholas. 'The jemmy is wearing out.'

'I'll get you a new one,' said Colin.

Nicholas went on reading. 'Simmer slowly. Take the eel from the pan and put under the grill. Pass the remaining liquor through butter muslin and reduce until it begins to adhere to the spoon. Sieve once again, pour over the eel and cook for two more minutes. Arrange the eel in the puff pastry with a border of grilled mushrooms. Decorate the centre with soft carp's roes. Garnish with the rest of the sauce that you have kept back.'

'Sounds delicious,' nodded Colin. 'I think Chick ought to enjoy that.'

'I haven't had the pleasure of meeting Mr Chick yet, sir,' concluded Nicholas, 'but if he doesn't like it, then I'll make something different next time and that will help me to plot more accurately an approximate graph of his likes and dislikes.'

'Hrumm . . . !' said Colin. 'I'll let you get on with it, Nicholas. I'll be laying the table.'

He went back through the corridor in the other direction, crossed the hall and ended up in the dining-room-cum-studio, whose pale blue carpet and pink beige walls were a treat for sore eyes.

The room, approximately twelve feet by fifteen, had two wide bay windows overlooking Armstrong Avenue. Large panes of glass kept the sounds of the avenue from the room, but let in the breath of springtime when it appeared outside. A limed oak table filled one corner of the room. There were wall seats at right angles to each other on two sides of it, and matching chairs with blue morocco upholstery on the other two sides. There were two other long low cupboards in the room – one fitted up as a record-player and record container with all the latest gadgets, and the other, identical with the first, containing catapults, cutlery, plates, glasses and other implements used by civilized society for eating.

Colin selected a light blue tablecloth to match the carpet. He decorated the centre of the table with a pharmaceutical jar in which a pair of embryonic chickens seemed to be dancing Nijinsky's choreography for *The Spectre of the Rose*. Around it he arranged some branches of bootlace mimosa – the gardener who worked for some friends of his had cultivated this by grafting strips of those black liquorice ribbons sold by haberdashers when school is over onto ordinary bobbled mimosa. Then for himself and his guest he took some white china plates with filigree designs in gold and stainless steel knives and forks with perforated handles inside each of which a stuffed ladybird, floating between two layers of perspex, brought good luck every time they were used. He added crystal goblets and servi-ettes folded into bishops' mitres; this took him quite a time. He had hardly finished all this when the bell sprang off the wall to let him know that Chick had arrived.

Colin smoothed out an imaginary crease in the table-cloth and went to open the door.

'How are you?' asked Chick.

'How are *you*?' replied Colin. 'Take off your mac and come and see what Nicholas has made for us.'

'Is he your new cook?'

'Yes,' said Colin. 'I swapped him at the pawnbroker's for a couple of pounds of Algerian coffee and the old one.'

'And is he any good?' asked Chick.

'He seems to know what he's doing. He swears by ffroydde.'

'What have sex and dreams got to do with cooking?' asked Chick, horrified. His lush black moustache began to droop at a tragic angle.

'No, you idiot, I'm talking about Saint Clement, not Monsignor Sigmund!'

'Oh, sorry!' said Chick. 'But you know I never read any-thing except Jean Pulse Heartre.'

He followed Colin into the tiled corridor, stroked the mice and casually scooped up a handful of sundrops to pop into his lighter.

'Nicholas,' said Colin as he went in, 'this is my friend Chick.'

'How do you do, sir?' said Nicholas.

'How do you do, Nicholas?' replied Chick. 'Haven't you got a niece called Alyssum?'

'Yes, sir,' said Nicholas. 'And a very pretty girl too, if I may be allowed to say so.'

'She looks very much like you,' said Chick. 'Although there are one or two differences around the bust . . .'

'I'm fairly broad, sir,' said Nicholas, 'but she is better developed in a perpendicular direction, if Mr Chick will permit the precision.'

'Well,' said Colin, 'it's almost a family reunion. You never told me you had a niece, Nicholas.'

'Ah! My sister went wrong, sir,' said Nicholas. 'She took up philosophy. It isn't the kind of thing we like to talk about outside the family . . .'

'Hm . . .' said Colin, 'I suppose you're right. At any rate, I see what you mean. Now, let's have a look at your Stiletto-toed Eel . . .'

'It would be fatal to open the cooker now,' warned Nicholas. 'By introducing air with a less rich water content than that already in the oven, desiccation would almost certainly take place.'

'I'd rather,' said Chick, 'have the pleasure of seeing it for the first time on the table.'

'Mr Chick's patience meets with my entire approval, sir,' said Nicholas. 'May I be allowed to beg Mr Colin's leave, sir, to continue with my good work?'

'Do carry on, please, Nicholas!'

Nicholas went back to the job he was doing when they had interrupted him. He was taking fillets of sole in truffled aspic out of their moulds. Their ultimate fate was to garnish the seafood hors d'oeuvres.

'Would you like a drink first?' asked Colin. 'I've finished my clavicocktail and we could try it out.'

'Does it really work?' asked Chick. 'Or do you have to wind it up with a harpsicorkscrew first?'

'Of course it works. I had a hard job getting it right, but the finished result is beyond my wildest dreams. When I played the "Black and Tan Fantasy" I got a really crazy concoction.'

'How does it work?' asked Chick.

'For each note,' said Colin, 'there's a corresponding drink – either a wine, spirit, liqueur or fruit juice. The loud pedal puts in egg flip and the soft pedal adds ice. For soda you play a cadenza in F sharp. The quantities depend on how long a note is held – you get the sixteenth of a measure for a hemidemisemiquaver; a whole measure for a black note; and four measures for a semibreve. When you play a slow tune, then tone comes into control too to prevent the amounts growing too large and the drink getting too big for a cocktail – but the alcoholic content remains unchanged. And, depending on the length of the tune, you can, if you like, vary the measures used, reducing them, say, to a hundredth in order to get a drink taking advantage of all the harmonics by means of an adjustment on the side.'

'Sounds a bit complicated,' said Chick.

'The whole thing is controlled by electrical contacts and relays. I won't go into all the technicalities because you know all about them anyway. And, anyway, the keyboard itself can work independently.'

'It's wonderful!' said Chick.

'Only one thing still worries me,' said Colin, 'and that's the loud pedal and the egg flip. I had to put in a special gear system because if you play something too hot, lumps of omelette fall into the glass, and they're rather hard to swallow. I've still got a few modifications to make there. But it's all right if you're careful. And if you feel like a dash of fresh cream, you add a chord in G major.'

'I'm going to try an improvisation on "Loveless Love",' said Chick. 'That should be fantastic.'

'It's still in the junk room that I use as my workshop,' said Colin, 'because the guard plates aren't screwed down yet. Come in there with me. I'll set it for two cocktails of about seventy-five milligallons each to start with.'

Chick sat at the instrument. When he'd reached the end of the tune a section of the front panel came down with a sharp click and a row of glasses appeared. Two of them were brimming with an appetizing mixture.

'You scared me,' said Colin. 'You played a wrong note once. Luckily it was only in the harmonization.'

'You don't mean to say that that comes into it too?' said Chick.

'Not always,' said Colin. 'That would make it too elaborate. So we just give it a few passing acknowledgements. Now drink up – and we'll go and eat.'

2

'This Stilettoed Eel is terrific,' said Chick. 'Where did you get the idea from?'

'Nicholas had it,' said Colin. 'There's an eel – or there *was* an eel, rather – that used to go into his wash-basin every day through the cold-water tap.'

'What a funny thing to do,' said Chick. 'Why did it do that?'

'It used to pop its head out and empty the toothpaste by squeezing the tube with its teeth. Nicholas only uses that American brand with the pineapple flavour, and I don't think it could resist the temptation.'

'How did he catch it?' asked Chick.

'One day he put a whole pineapple there instead of the toothpaste. When it was only the tube it would suck out the toothpaste, swallow it, and then pop its head straight back. But with the pineapple it wouldn't work. The harder it pulled, the farther its teeth sunk in. Nicholas . . .'

Colin held back the rest of his sentence.

'Nicholas what?' said Chick.

'I'm scared to tell you the rest. It might take away your appetite.'

'Carry on,' said Chick, 'my plate's almost empty, anyway.'

'Well, Nicholas came in at that very moment and sliced off its head with a razor blade. Then he swiftly turned on the tap and out came the rest.'

'Is that all?' said Chick. 'Give me some more then! I hope it left a large family in the tank.'

'Nicholas has put out a tube of raspberry-flavoured toothpaste to see . . .' said Colin. 'But tell me more about this Alyssum you were talking to him about . . .'

'I can just see her now,' said Chick. 'I met her at one of Jean Pulse's lectures. We were both lying flat on our stomachs under the platform – and that's how I got to know her . . .'

'What's she like?'

'Oh, I'm no good at descriptions,' said Chick. 'She's pretty . . .'

'Ah! . . .' said Colin.

Nicholas came back. He was bringing in the turkey.

'Sit down and eat with us, Nicholas,' said Colin. 'After all, as Chick was saying, you're almost one of the family.'

'I must see to the mice first, if Mr Colin has no objections, sir,' said Nicholas. 'But I'll be back in a moment. I've already carved the turkey . . . And here is the sauce . . .'

'Wait till you taste it,' said Colin. 'It's a sauce made from creamed mangoes and juniper berries piped into little pouches of plaited veal. You blow into them like bagpipes and the sauce comes out like toothpaste.'

'Super!' said Chick.

'You wouldn't like to give me some clues about the way in which you entered into your relationship with her? . . .' Colin went on.

'Well . . .' said Chick, 'I asked her if she liked Jean Pulse Heartre and she told me that she collected all his works . . . Then I said to her "So do I" . . . And every time that I said something to her, she answered "So do I", and vice versa . . . Then, finally, just as an existentialist experiment, I said to her "I love you very much". But that time she just said "Oh!" . . .'

'So the experiment was a flop,' said Colin.

'I suppose so,' said Chick. 'But all the same she didn't go. So then I said "I'm going that way", and she said "I'm not". But she went on "I'm going *this* way" . . .'

'Extraordinary,' nodded Colin.

'So I said "So am I" . . .' said Chick. 'And after that I went everywhere that she did . . .'

'And the consequence was? . . .' said Colin.

'Hmmm! . . .' said Chick. 'Well, it was bedtime . . .'

Colin gulped hard and swallowed down a bottle of red wine before he recovered.

'I'm going skating with her tomorrow,' said Chick. 'It's Sunday. How about coming with us? We're going in the morning because there won't be too many people around then. I'm not all that keen,' he remarked, 'because I'm a rotten skater, but we can always talk about Heartre.'

'I'll be there . . .' promised Colin. 'And I'll bring Nicholas . . . Maybe he's got some more nieces . . .'

3

Colin stepped down from the tube train and went up the escalator. He came out on the wrong side of the station, turned left and went right round it before he could get his bearings. He used his yellow silk handkerchief to find out the direction of the wind. It immediately swept all the colour out of the handkerchief and spread it over a large lumpy building which suddenly took on the appearance of the Rinkspot Skating Club.

The bump on the side nearest Colin was the indoor swimming pool. He went past that, and on the other side penetrated into the petrified organism by going through a double set of plate glass swing doors with bronze handles. When he showed his season ticket to the Commissionaire it winked at him through the two little round holes that had already been punched in it. The Commissionaire smiled back, but nevertheless gave a third brutal punch to the orange card and the ticket was blinded for life. Colin hurriedly put it back into his wallodile crocket and turned left into a corridor with a rubber floor that led to the changing cubicles. The ones at the level of the rink were all full. So he went up the concrete stairs, bumping into some very tall people on their way down cutting extraordinary capers and trying desperately to behave naturally despite the obvious disadvantage of being perched on vertical metallic blades. A man in a white polo-necked sweater opened a cubicle for him, pocketed the tip Colin gave him for his pains but which Colin was sure he would spend on pleasure because he looked like a liar, and left Colin to rest in peace there alone, after having carelessly scribbled his initials with a piece of chalk on a little blackboard specially put there for that purpose. Colin noticed that the man did not have a man's head, but an ostrich's, and couldn't understand why he was working in the ice-rink instead of at the swimming pool.

An oval sound rose from the rink, overlaid by the music of loud-speakers scattered all around. The skaters' trampling had not yet reached the sonic booming of those hectic moments when the noise it makes can be compared to a regiment marching over cobbled roads through squelching mud. Colin looked round for Alyssum and Chick, but they did not seem to be on the ice. Nicholas was coming to join him a little later; he still had some work to do in the kitchen in preparation for lunch.

Colin undid his shoelaces and noticed that his soles had gone. He took a roll of sticky tape from his pocket, but there wasn't enough left. So he planted his shoes in a little puddle of condensation on the concrete seat and sprinkled them with concentrated fertilizer to make the leather sprout again quickly. He slipped on a pair of thick woollen socks with wide yellow and purple stripes, and put on his skating boots. His skates had blades that were divided in two at the front so that he could easily make changes of direction.

BORIS VIAN

He went out of his cubicle, and downstairs again. His
ankles twisted slightly on the corrugated rubber that lined
the reinforced concrete corridors. Just as he was about to
risk himself on the rink he had to spring back to avoid
being knocked over. A skating draughtswoman, at the end
of a magnificent whirlwind spread eagle (which she termed
a double elephant), laid an enormous egg which split open
at Colin's feet.

While one of the serf-sweepers was cleaning up the scattered fragments, Colin noticed Chick and Alyssum who had
just arrived on the other side of the rink. He waved at them,
but as they did not see him he set off to meet them without
taking the gyratory movement of the rink into account. The
result was the rapid formation of a tremendous heap of
people rushing to complain. Every second they were joined
by a vast agglomeration of others, desperately beating their
arms, their legs, their shoulders and their whole bodies in
the air before collapsing on to the pile of the first fallen. As
the sun had melted the surface of the ice, there was a horrible squelching under the heap of bodies.

In no time at all ninety per cent of the skaters were on
the heap and Chick and Alyssum had the rink to themselves – or almost. They went up to the swarming mass and
Chick, recognizing Colin by his cleft skates, grabbed his
ankles and extricated him from the seething crowd. They
shook hands. Chick introduced Alyssum and Colin put
himself on her left as Chick already occupied the dexter
flank.

They brushed themselves down when they reached the
far side of the rink to make room for the serf-sweepers who,
giving up all hope of finding anything but worthless rags
and tatters of disconnected personalities in the mountain

16

of victims, had got out their squeegees to wipe out the hundreds of stiffs, and shoved them into the gully while singing the Rinkunabulan Anthem composed by Beatrice Webb in 1892, and which goes something like this:

Withdraw, sweet skaters, from the icy scene –
Within a trice the serfs will sweep it clean . . .

The whole ceremony was punctuated with exclamation marks from the whooter which were intended to instil, in the depths of the most devoted souls, a shudder of incoercible terror.

Those skaters who were left applauded the initiative that had been shown, and the trap closed over the rest. Chick, Alyssum and Colin said a short prayer and began to gyrate once again.

Colin looked at Alyssum. By some strange trick of Fate she was wearing a white tee-shirt with a yellow skirt. She had white and yellow shoes, with ice-hockey skates. She had smoked silk stockings and short white socks rolled over the tops of her little boots whose fluffy white laces had been twisted three times round her ankles. On top of all this she also had a sharp green silk scarf and masses of thick blonde hair from which her face peeped out. She looked out at the world through wide open blue eyes, and the boundaries of her being were delineated by a skin that was radiant and golden. She possessed round arms and calves, a narrow waist and a bust that was so perfect it might have been a photo.

Colin looked somewhere else in order to steady himself. When he had managed this he lowered his eyes and asked Chick if the Stilettoed Eel hadn't given him indigestion.

'Don't talk to me about it,' said Chick. 'I stayed up all night fishing in my bathroom to see if I could find one too. But there only seems to be trout in my place.'

'Nicholas ought to be able to do something for you,' said Colin, reassuringly. And then, addressing himself more particularly to Alyssum, 'You have an extraordinarily gifted uncle.'

'He's the pride of the family,' said Alyssum. 'My mother's never got over being married to a mathematical wizard with nothing more than a first in calculus while her brother has done so well for himself in life.'

'Your father's a wizard with a degree in maths?'

'Yes, he's a don at the University and a member of the Magic Squared Circle . . .' said Alyssum. 'It's awful. And he's thirty-eight! You'd think he might have made some effort. Luckily we've always got Uncle Nicholas.'

'Wasn't he going to come this morning?' said Chick.

A heady perfume rose from Alyssum's shining hair. Colin moved away a little.

'I think he's going to be late. He was full of inspiration this morning . . . If you'd both like to come back home for lunch with me, we'll find out what it was . . .'

'Fine,' said Chick. 'But if you think I'm going to accept an invitation like that, then you must have a very strange conception of the Universe . . . Find a fourth first! I'm not going to let Alyssum go to your place or you'll seduce her with the magic of your clavicocktail – and I'm not standing for that.'

'Oh . . .' protested Colin. 'Hark at the things he's saying! . . .'

He didn't hear any more because an inordinately lengthy individual, who had been giving a demonstration of speed for the past five minutes, had just slipped through his legs by leaning forward as far as possible and the rush of air that he created lifted Colin several yards above the ground. He clutched the edge of the first floor gallery, got his balance and after doing a backwards somersault the wrong way round, landed back at the sides of Chick and Alyssum.

'They ought to be stopped from going too fast,' said Colin.

Then he quickly crossed himself because the culprit had just skated straight into the wall of the restaurant at the other end of the rink and flattened himself against it like a marshmallow jellyfish picked to pieces by a destructive child.

The serf-sweepers once again did their duty and one of them planted a cross of ice on the spot where the accident had occurred. As it melted, the Master of Ceremonies played a selection of religious records.

Then everything went back to normal. And Chick, Alyssum and Colin went round and round and round.

4

'Here's Nicholas!' cried Alyssum.

'And there's Isis!' said Chick.

Nicholas had just turned up at the pay-desk, and Isis had just appeared in the rink. The former went to the upper floors; the latter to join Chick, Colin and Alyssum.

'Hallo, Isis,' said Colin. 'This is Alyssum. Alyssum, this is Isis. You know Chick.'

There were handshakes all round and Chick made the

most of this to slip away with Alyssum, leaving Isis in Colin's arms, in which position they both immediately took off.

'It's nice to see you again,' said Isis.

Colin thought it was nice to see her again too. During her eighteen years of life Isis had managed to equip herself with chestnut hair, a white tee-shirt and a yellow skirt with a sharp green scarf, white and yellow shoes and a pair of sunglasses. She was pretty. But Colin knew her parents very well.

'There's a tea-party at our place next week,' said Isis. 'It's Wry-Tangle's birthday.'

'Who's Wry-Tangle?'

'My poodle. So I'm asking all my friends round. You'll come, won't you? Will four be all right? . . .'

'Of course,' said Colin. 'I'd love to come.'

'Bring your friends too!' said Isis.

'Chick and Alyssum?'

'Yes, they're nice . . . See you on Sunday then!'

'Are you going already?' said Colin.

'Yes. I never stay anywhere long. And I've already been here since ten o'clock, you know . . .'

'But it's only eleven!' said Colin.

'Ah, but I was in the bar! . . . See you! . . .'

5

Colin hurried through the glistening streets. The wind was keen and dry, and little patches of ice snapped, crackled and popped underfoot.

People hid behind anything they could find – the collars

of their overcoats, their scarves, their muffs – and he even saw one man who had wrapped himself in a gilded bird-cage with its little door pressing down on his nose.

'I'm going to the High-Pottinuice's tomorrow,' thought Colin.

That was Isis's parents' name.

'And tonight I'm having supper with Chick . . .

'I'll go back home to get ready for tomorrow . . .'

He took a big step to avoid a join in the pavement that looked particularly dangerous.

'If I can do twenty steps without walking on the joints,' said Colin, 'I won't get a pimple on my nose tomorrow.'

'But it won't make any difference,' he said, jumping on to the ninth joint with both feet, 'because that kind of superstition is stupid. I won't get a pimple whatever I do.'

He bent down to pick a pink and blue orchid that the frost had brought out of the earth.

It smelt like Alyssum's hair.

'I'll be seeing Alyssum tomorrow . . .'

But that was something he shouldn't think about. Legally Alyssum belonged to Chick.

'I'm bound to find a girl tomorrow . . .'

But his thoughts still lingered on Alyssum.

'Do they really discuss Jean Pulse Heartre when they're alone? . . .'

But perhaps it was best not to think about what they did when they were alone together.

'How many articles has Jean Pulse Heartre written during the last year? . . .'

At any rate, there wasn't enough time for him to count them all before he got home.

'I wonder what Nicholas is making for this evening . . .'

When you came to think about it, the likeness between Alyssum and Nicholas wasn't all that extraordinary since they both belonged to the same family. He was slyly creeping back to the forbidden topic and he quickly thought about something else.

'How I wonder what Nicholas – who is so much like Alyssum – is making for this evening . . .'

'Nicholas is eleven years older than Alyssum. That makes him twenty-nine. He's a tremendously gifted cook. He's going to make a casserole.'

Colin was almost home.

'Flower-shops never have shutters. Nobody ever thinks of stealing flowers.'

That was logical enough. He picked a grey and orange orchid with a delicate trembling tendril. Its colours shimmered in the light like shot silk.

'It's just like the mouse with the black whiskers . . . And I'm home!'

Colin went up the stone staircase that was wrapped in its thick winter woollies. Into the lock in the door of silvered glass he introduced a little golden key.

'Hither, my faithful lackeys! . . . Your master is returned! . . .'

He flung his mac on to a chair and went to look for Nicholas.

6

'Nicholas, are you going to make a casserole tonight?' asked Colin.

'Good Lord,' said Nicholas, 'Mr Colin didn't ask me to. I'd thought of something quite different.'

'Caterwauling cockleshells!' said Colin. 'Why must you always talk to me perpetually in the third person?'

'If Mr Colin will give me permission to explain my reasons, sir, I should like to state that I find any familiarity permissible only after the barriers have been consistently respected on both sides – and that certainly is not the case here.'

'You're a bloody snob, Nicholas,' said Colin.

'I have the pride of my position, sir,' said Nicholas, 'and you can't complain about that.'

'Of course not,' said Colin. 'But I wish you weren't always so aloof.'

'I have a sincere affection for Mr Colin underneath, sir,' said Nicholas.

'And I'm proud of it – and happy too, Nicholas – and I feel just the same about you. Therefore . . . what are you going to make tonight?'

'Once again I shall remain within the ffroyddian tradition by making musk-antler bangers with port and mash.'

'And how are you going to do that?' said Colin.

'This is the recipe. Take a bunch of musk-antler bangers and skin them, taking no heed whatsoever of their screams. Carefully preserve the skins. Alternate rounds of the musk-antler bangers with sliced lobster claws that have been previously tossed in hot butter. Place them on ice in a pan. Heighten the flame and, in the space thereby gained, tastefully arrange little rings of coddled rice. When the bangers emit a continuous low note, take them swiftly from the flame and cover with rare old tawny port. Stir in with a platinum spatula. Grease a tin to prevent it rusting and then line it with the bangers. Just before serving, make a thick sauce of periwinkles, parsley and a pint of pure cream. Sprinkle with valerian drops, garnish with the rice rings, serve . . . and disappear.'

'I'm starving,' said Colin. 'I can't wait. Your ffroyde is a genius. But tell me, Nicholas, do you think it will make me get a pimple on my nose tomorrow?'

Nicholas gave great consideration to the condition of Colin's conk and concluded that it would not.

'Oh, and while I'm on the subject, do you know how to do the Squint?'

'My technical development hasn't advanced much beyond the Disraeli Dislocation and the Aurora Borealis which were still the rage last week in Swingingsville,' said Nicholas, 'so I haven't perfected all the refinements of the Squint. But I certainly know the rudiments of the dance.'

'Do you think,' asked Colin, 'that its technique could be mastered in one evening?'

'I should think so,' said Nicholas. 'The basic movements aren't very complicated. All one has to do is avoid vulgar faux-pas and errors of taste, such as trying to dance the Squint to a boogie-woogie.'

'That would be wrong? . . .'

'It would be a serious crime against good taste!'

Nicholas put the grapefruit that he had been peeling during this interview on to the table and his hands under the tap.

'Are you very busy?' asked Colin.

'Good Lord, no, sir,' said Nicholas. 'Everything in the kitchen is going along nicely.'

'Then perhaps you would be so kind as to instruct me

in the rudiments of the Squint,' said Colin. 'Come into the other room and I'll put on a record.'

'I would like to advise Mr Colin, sir, to choose something with feeling – something like "Chloe" in an arrangement by Duke Ellington, or the "Concerto for Johnny Hodges" . . .' said Nicholas. 'Something that they might call sultry or moody on the other side of the Atlantic.'

7

'The principle of the Squint,' said Nicholas, 'as Mr Colin no doubt knows, sir, relies on the simultaneous setting-up of interferences obtained via the rigorously synchronized oscillatory movements of two loosely connected centres of animation.'

'I didn't realize,' said Colin, 'that it was concerned with such advanced developments in physics.'

'In this case,' said Nicholas, 'the dancer and his partner should attempt to maintain the minimum perceptible distance between themselves. Then their entire bodies begin to vibrate following the rhythm of the music.'

'You don't say,' said Colin, looking slightly worried.

'A series of static undulations is then set up,' said Nicholas, 'presenting, as in the laws of acoustics, various diaphragmatic vibrations and frictions which make a large contribution to the creation of the right atmosphere on a dance-floor.'

'Naturally . . .' murmured Colin.

'Experts in the Squint,' pursued Nicholas, 'sometimes succeed in producing subsidiary layers of subordinate waves by setting certain selected limbs and members of their anatomies into separately synchronized vibration. But we needn't go into that now . . . I'll simply try to show Mr Colin how they do it.'

Colin chose 'Chloe', as Nicholas had suggested its suitability, and carefully centred it on the turntable of the record-player. He delicately dropped the point of the needle into the very bottom of the beginning of the first groove and watched Nicholas gradually start to shake.

8

'Mr Colin will soon get it, sir!' said Nicholas. 'Just one more time.'

'But why,' asked Colin, covered in perspiration, 'must it be done to a slow tune? It's much more difficult that way.'

'There is a reason,' said Nicholas. 'Theoretically the dancer and his partner should keep at the minimum distance from each other. With a slow tune, the undulations can be regulated in such a way that the point of maximum coincidence is situated roughly half-way up each partner, while their extremities are at liberty to improvise separate movements. That is the result that should be aimed at in theory. But unfortunately it has happened that, in practice, unscrupulous couples have tried dancing the Squint the way the coloured kids do it – to a quick tempo.'

'Which means?' asked Colin.

'Which means that with alternating centres of gravity at bottom and top, and another intermediate mobile nodal point regrettably situated in the region of the loins, the fixed points – or pseudo-articulations – become the sternum and the knees.'

Colin blushed.

'I see,' he said.

'When this is done to a boogie rhythm,' concluded Nicholas, 'the obscenity of the dance generally dominates the hypnotic qualities of the music.'

Colin was in a trance.

'Where did you learn the Squint?' he asked Nicholas.

'My niece taught me . . .' said Nicholas. 'I worked out the complete theory of the Squint during a series of talks with my brother-in-law. He's a practising Pythagorean, as Mr Colin is no doubt aware, sir, and did not find it very difficult to follow the method of the system. He even told me that he had calculated its principles nineteen years ago . . .'

'. . . Your niece is eighteen, isn't she?' asked Colin.

'And three months . . .' corrected Nicholas. 'Now if Mr Colin doesn't need my services any more, sir, I'll go back to have a look at what's cooking in the kitchen.'

'Run along, Nicholas. And thanks,' said Colin, taking off the record that had just finished playing.

9

'I think I'll put on my camel suit and my noon-blue shirt, my tie with the scarlet and Sahara stripes, my punched suede shoes and my nasturtium and dromedary striped socks.

'But first of all I'll give myself a wash and a shave and a check-up to make sure that there's nothing missing.

27

'Then I'll go and say to Nicholas in the kitchen "Nicholas, how would you like to come to a dance with me?"'

'Good Lord,' said Nicholas, 'if Mr Colin insists, then I shall have no alternative but to go. But if he should not insist, sir, then I should be delighted to take the opportunity to put several outstanding matters in order, the urgency of which is becoming imperative.'

'Would it be indiscreet of me, Nicholas, if I were to ask you what the hell you were talking about?'

'I am President,' said Nicholas, 'of the District Housekeepers Philosophical Society, and consequently am compelled to attend the maximum number of meetings that it holds.'

'Dare I ask, Nicholas, what the subject of today's meeting is going to be?'

'We shall be discussing commitment. One of our members has discovered a connection between the various forms of commitment, beginning with Jean Pulse Heartre's conception and then going on to the commitment of suicides, commitment to total abstinence, commitment to prison, to the flames, to memory, to writing, to a lunatic asylum – or commitment to duty – in particular, by housekeepers.'

'Chick would be very interested in that!' said Colin.

'I'm extremely sorry,' said Nicholas, 'but the membership is very limited. We couldn't possibly let Mr Chick come in. Housekeepers only, I'm afraid, sir.'

'Nicholas,' asked Colin, 'why do you always give them that ambiguous title?'

'No doubt Mr Colin will have noticed,' said Nicholas, 'that whereas it might remain comparatively harmless to refer to a gentleman keeping house as a housemaster, it would be very unseemly to speak similarly of a lady as a mistress. Therefore we choose to have a designation that embraces us all . . .'

'You're quite right, of course, Nicholas. Now, in your opinion, do you think I'm likely to meet my soulmate today? . . . I'd like to meet one exactly identical to your niece . . .'

'Mr Colin is making a grave mistake in thinking so much about my niece, sir,' said Nicholas, 'since from the accounts of recent events it would appear that Mr Chick has chosen her first.'

'Oh, but Nicholas,' said Colin, 'I do so much want to be in love . . .'

A puff of steam sprang out of the spout of the kettle and Nicholas went to open the door. The caretaker had brought up two letters.

'Is there some mail?' said Colin.

'I'm sorry, sir,' said Nicholas, 'but they're both for me. Is Mr Colin expecting a letter?'

'I wish a pretty girl would write to me,' said Colin. 'That's all I was hoping for.'

'It's lunchtime,' concluded Nicholas. 'Would Mr Colin like his breakfast now? There's minced oxtail, a bowl of spiced punch, and anchovy butter on toast.'

'Nicholas, why won't Chick bring your niece home here to lunch unless I invite another girl too?'

'Mr Colin must forgive me, sir,' said Nicholas, 'but under the circumstances, I would do exactly the same. Mr Colin is a very good-looking fellow . . .'

'Nicholas,' said Colin, 'if I'm not in love by this evening – really and truly in love – then I'll start a collection of the works of the Marchioness Thighbone de Mauvoir . . . and see if some of my friend Chick's luck rubs off on me!'

10

'I wish I were in love,' said Colin. 'The butcher-boy wishes he were in love. And the baker-boy wishes exactly ditto (i.e. that he were in love). The candlestick-maker's-boy and everybody in the street wishes and wishes that I were and they were and you were and we were and that the whole wide world were too. And even those that are left wish that they could fall in love as well . . .'

He was tying his tie in front of the bathroom mirror. 'All I have to do now is put on my jacket, my overcoat and my scarf, then my right glove followed by my left glove. But I won't have to put on my hat because I don't want to spoil my hair. Hey, what are you doing there?'

He made this last remark to the little grey mouse with the black whiskers who was certainly far from home, nonchalantly leaning on its elbows over the rim of the tooth-glass.

'Just suppose,' he said, sitting on the edge of the bath (rectangular, and made of yellow vitreous enamel) in order to get closer to the mouse, 'that I should meet my old friend Whatsisname at the High-Pottinuice's . . . !'

The mouse nodded understandingly.

'And suppose . . . Well, why not? . . . that he should have a pretty little cousin . . . dressed in a white tee-shirt, with a yellow skirt . . . and that her name was Aly . . . Baba . . .'

The mouse uncrossed its paws and looked shocked.

'It's not a very pretty name for a girl, I know,' said Colin. 'But then you're a sweet little mouse – and yet you've got black whiskers. So . . . ?'

He stood up.

'It's three o'clock already! Look, you're making me late. Chick and . . . I mean Chick is bound to get there very early.'

He wetted his finger and held it up over his head, then brought it down again very smartly. It was burnt as severely as if he had put it in the fire.

'There's love in the air,' he decided. 'It's boiling! I stand up, the butcher-boy stands up, the baker-boy stands up. And with the candlestick-maker's-boy we all stand up, stand up, stand up. Do you want to be helped out of the glass?'

The mouse proved that it needed help from nobody by scrambling out on its own and nibbling off a lolly-shaped piece of soap for itself.

'Don't make a mess over everything with that,' said Colin. 'You're disgustingly greedy.'

He went out of the bathroom and into the bedroom and slipped on his jacket, picked himself up, and put it on.

'Nicholas must have gone . . . He must know some crazy girls . . . They say that all the girls where he comes from go to work as maids of practically all trades for philosophers . . .'

He closed the bedroom door behind him.

'There's a slight tear in the lining of my left sleeve . . . And there's no insulating tape left . . . Too bad, I'll use a nail.'

The flat door slammed behind him with a noise like a naked hand slapping a bare bottom . . . He began to tremble . . .

'I must think of something else . . . Suppose I break my neck going down the stairs . . .'

The staircase carpet – very pale mauve – only showed signs of wear on every third tread because Colin always went down four at a time. He caught his feet in a chromium stairrod and became entangled in the banisters.

'That'll teach me to think nonsense. Serves me right. I am stupid, the butcher-boy is stupid, the . . .'

There was pain in his back. He understood why when he

BORIS VIAN

reached the bottom and threw away the banister that was
sticking out from the back of his overcoat collar.

The street door closed behind him with a sound that was
like a kiss on an uncovered shoulder.

'What is there to see in the street?'

First of all there were two road-menders playing cricket.
The fattest one's belly wobbled up and down contrapun-
tally as its owner jumped down and up. For a ball they had
a crucifix painted red with the cross missing.

Colin walked on.

To right and left rose elegant and fantastic mud-huts
with large bay windows. A woman was leaning out of one of
them. Colin blew her a kiss and she shook on his head the
hearthrug of black and silver swansdown that her husband
couldn't stand.

Shops brightened up the stark appearance of the big
buildings. A display of supplies for fakirs caught Colin's
attention. He noted that the price of broken glass and long
nails had gone up since last week.

He passed a dog and two other people. People were
being kept indoors by the cold. Those who managed to
tear themselves from its clutches escaped minus most of
their clothes and died of pneumonia.

The traffic policeman at the crossroads had hidden
his head in his cape. He looked like a big black umbrella.
Waiters from the cafés ran round him in circles to keep
themselves warm.

A boy and a girl were kissing in a doorway.

'Don't let me see them . . . Don't . . . Don't let me see
them . . . They're driving me mad.'

Colin crossed over. A boy and a girl were kissing in a
doorway.

He closed his eyes and began to run.

He opened them again very quickly because, under his eyelids, he could see thousands and thousands of girls going round – and such a vision would make him lose his way. There was still one right in front of him, walking in the same direction. You could see her pretty legs in little white lamb bootees under her coat of unglazed panda-skin and her matching hat. Red hair under the hat. Her coat flew out from her shoulders and danced all round her as she walked.

'I must overtake her. I must see her face . . .'

He got ahead of her and burst into tears. She was at least fifty-nine. He sat on the kerb until the tears stopped flowing. It made him feel a lot better. With a little crackle his tears froze and shattered like glass as they fell on to the hard granite pavement.

After five minutes or so he realized that he was sitting in front of Isis High-Pottinuice's house. A pair of girls walked past him and went straight in.

His heart swelled up to ten times its normal size, became completely weightless, lifted him up above the earth, and he went straight in after them.

11

A rumble of sounds from the party being thrown upstairs by Isis's parents could already be heard from the first floor. The staircase spiralled round three times, thereby trebling any sounds that ventured into it, each stair acting like a tiny fin in the cylindrical sound-box of the vibes. Colin went up, with his head close on the heels of the pair of girls. Pretty reinforced heels of flesh-coloured nylon, high-heeled shoes of fine leather, and slender delicate ankles. Then the seams of the stockings, imperceptibly meandering, like fabulously long slinky caterpillars leading to the articulated concave curves between suspender and knee. Colin stopped to let them get two steps ahead, then he set off again. From his new position he could see the tops of their stockings, the extra thickness there, and the shadowy whiteness of the thighs of the one on the left. The other girl's skirt, tightly pleated, did not allow him such advantageous views, but under her beaver-lamb coat her hips swivelled with greater symmetry than those of the first girl, making another little rival pleat . . . Out of decency Colin began to look down at his feet, and watched them as they arrived at the second floor.

He was right behind the pair of girls just as they were being let in.

'Hallo, Colin!' said Isis. 'How are you?' He drew her towards him and kissed her between her hair and her cheek. Her perfume was tantalizing.

'But it isn't *my* birthday!' she protested. 'It's Wry-Tangle's! . . .'

'Where is Wry-Tangle? I want to congratulate him! . . .'

'Isn't it disgusting,' said Isis. 'This morning we took him to the trimmer's to have his coat clipped and make him handsome. They gave him a bath and the whole treatment . . . And then at two o'clock three of his friends came round with four bundles of horrible old bones and off he went with them. He's bound to come back in a terrible state! . . .'

'It is *his* birthday, after all,' frowned Colin.

Through the opening between the double doors he

could see the other boys and girls. A dozen of them were dancing, but most of the others were standing close to each other, with their hands behind their backs, in pairs of the same sex, exchanging extremely unconvincing impressions with even more unconvincing expressions.

'Take off your coat,' said Isis. 'Follow me and I'll show you the way to the boys' cloakroom.'

He followed her, squeezing past another pair of girls who were emerging, in the opposite direction, along with the compacted sounds of snapping bags and puffing powder, from Isis's bedroom which had been transformed into a girls' cloakroom for the occasion. Iron hooks and rails, borrowed from the butcher's, hung from the ceiling, and as decorations Isis had also borrowed a couple of closely skinned sheep's heads to grin at the end of each row.

The boys' cloakroom, which had been set up in Isis's father's study, consisted solely of the suppression of all the furniture in the said room. One simply unwrapped one's carcass on the floor – and that was that. Colin gave a brilliant performance, but lingered for a second in front of a mirror.

'Come on! Hurry up!' said Isis impatiently. 'I want to take you to meet some really charming girls.'

He held both her wrists and drew her towards him.

'Your dress is a dream,' he said.

It was a simple little dress of almond-green cashmere, with great gilded ceramic buttons, and the low back was filled in with a wrought-iron portcullis.

'Do you like it?' said Isis.

'It's a dream of a dream,' said Colin. 'Can you put your hand through the bars without being bitten?'

'Better not try,' said Isis.

She broke loose, seized Colin's hand and dragged him to the centre of maximum perspiration. They elbowed their way past a sharp member of the sexy sex and a sexy member of the sharp sex who had just arrived, slipped round a corner of the corridor and reached the central fulcrum of fun by going through the dining-room door.

'Just a second! . . .' said Colin. 'Are Alyssum and Chick there already?'

'Of course,' said Isis. 'Come on, this is . . .'

Half the girls were presentable. One of them was wearing an almond-green cashmere dress with great buttons of gilded pottery and, in its low back, a modesty vest of the most unusual design.

'That's the one I want to meet first, please,' said Colin.

Isis shook him and told him to behave himself.

'Are you going to be a good boy, my lad? . . .'

But he already had his eyes on a different girl, and was dragging his guide towards her.

'This is Colin,' said Isis. 'Colin, this is Chloe.'

Colin took a tremendous gulp. His mouth felt as if it were stuffed with the frizzled crumbs of burnt doughnuts.

'Hallo!' said Chloe.

'Ha . . . Have you been put into an arrangement by Duke Ellington?' asked Colin . . . And then he ran away because he knew he had said something very silly.

Chick grabbed him by the flap on the back of his jacket.

'Where do you think you're going? You can't run away like that. Look what I've got! . . .'

He pulled a little book bound in red morocco out of his pocket.

'It's the first edition of Heartre's *Spewpuke Paradox* . . .'

'So you managed to find it at last?' said Colin.

Then he remembered that he was running away – and so he started to run again.

Alyssum stood in his way.

'Do you mean to say you're going home without even having one tiny little dance with me?' she said.

'I'm sorry,' said Colin, 'but I've just done something idiotic and I can't possibly stay any longer.'

'But if somebody looks at you like this, how can you possibly refuse?'

'Oh, Alyssum . . .' groaned Colin, putting his arm round her and nestling his cheek into her hair.

'What's the matter, my poor dear old Colin?'

'I've put my damned silly foot into it and ruined everything, blast it! See that girl there? . . .'

'You mean Chloe? . . .'

'Do you know her? . . .' said Colin. 'I said the silliest thing to her, and that's why I was running home.'

He did not add that it was as if one of those German brass bands where you can hear nothing but the big drums was playing at full blast inside his noon-blue shirt.

'She's pretty, isn't she?' said Alyssum.

Chloe had red lips, dark brown hair, a gay happy smile, and a dress that might just as well not have been there at all.

'I daren't answer you!' said Colin.

So he left Alyssum, and went to ask Chloe. She looked at him. And then laughed and put her hand on his shoulder. He felt her cool fingers against the back of his neck. He curtailed the distance between their two bodies by temporarily disembraining both heads of his right biceps which had just received a judiciously commissioned cranial communication.

Chloe went on looking at him. She shook her long silky hair out of her blue eyes, and with a firm gesture of determination applied her temples to Colin's cheek.

An enormous silence spread out around them, and the major part of the rest of the world faded into insignificance.

But, as they might have expected, the record came to an end. Then, and only then, did Colin come down to earth and notice that the ceiling was made of transparent perspex and that the people upstairs were looking down at them. A wide border of water-irises sealed off the bottoms of the walls, and variously coloured vapours were escaping here and there through specially made openings in the ceiling. He also noticed that his friend Isis was standing in front of him with some refreshments on an onyx platter.

'No thanks, Isis,' said Chloe, tossing her hair.

'Yes please, Isis,' said Colin, helping a toad out of the hole and himself to a finger of Welsh rarebit pie and a Bombay duck's egg.

'You should have taken some,' he said to Chloe. 'They're very good.'

And then he coughed because he had swallowed by mistake a hedgehog quill that was hidden in one of the delicacies.

Chloe laughed, and her pretty teeth glistened.

'What is it?'

He had to turn his back on her to finish choking and, in the end, he managed to stop. Chloe came back with two glasses.

'Drink this,' she said, 'it'll make you feel better.'

'Thanks,' said Colin. 'Is it champagne?'

'It's a kind of cocktail.'

He swallowed the whole glass and choked again. Chloe

couldn't stop laughing. Chick and Alyssum came up. 'What's the matter?' asked Chick.

'He doesn't know how to drink!' said Chloe.

Alyssum tapped him gently on the back and the echo sounded like a Balinese gong. Everybody immediately stopped dancing and went in to dinner.

'There we are,' said Chick. 'Now we're all quiet. How about putting on something really good? . . .'

He winked at Colin.

'Let's do the Squint!' suggested Alyssum.

Chick dug through the pile of records near the record-player.

'Dance with me, Chick,' Alyssum said to him.

'I've found something,' said Chick. 'Let's put it on.'

It was a boogie-woogie.

Chloe was waiting.

'You're not going to do the Squint to that, are you? . . .' said Colin, horrified.

'Why not? . . .' asked Chick.

'Don't look at them,' Colin said to Chloe.

He bent down his head and kissed her between the ear and shoulder. She trembled, but did not take her head away.

Colin did not take away his lips either.

Alyssum and Chick, however, gave themselves up, body and soul, to an outstanding display of the Squint – the way the coloured kids do it.

The record soon came to an end. Alyssum broke loose and looked for something to play next, while Chick dropped flat on to the divan in front of Colin and Chloe. He grabbed them by the legs and brought them tumbling down beside him.

'Well, my lambs,' he said, 'having fun?'

Colin sat up and Chloe snuggled up comfortably beside him.

'She's a lovely kid, isn't she?' said Chick.

Chloe smiled. Colin said nothing, but put his arm round Chloe's shoulders and absent-mindedly began to play with the top button of her dress – which opened down the front.

Alyssum came back.

'Move along, Chick. I want to sit between you and Colin.'

Her choice of record was highly appropriate. It was 'Chloe', arranged by Duke Ellington. Colin nibbled a corner of Chloe's hair just behind her ear. And murmured, 'It's you. It's you!'

And before Chloe could say anything, all the others came back to dance, having realized that it wasn't time for dinner after all.

'Oh! . . .' said Chloe. 'What a pity! . . .'

12

'Well, are you going to see her again?' asked Chick.

They were sitting down to Nicholas's latest creation – pumpkin and walnuts.

'I don't know,' said Colin. 'I don't know what to do. She's such a nice girl . . . Last time, when we were out with Isis, she drank an awful lot of champagne . . .'

'And it suited her marvellously,' said Chick. 'She's extremely pretty. Don't look so miserable! . . . Guess what I found today? A copy of Heartre's *Choice Before Eructation* printed on an unperforated toilet roll.'

'Fine. But where d'you get all the money from?' said Colin.

It was Chick's turn to look glum.

'It did cost me a lot, but I can't do without it,' he said. 'I need Heartre. I'm building up a collection and I must have everything he's done.'

'But he won't stop doing things,' said Colin. 'He writes at least five articles a week . . .'

'I know,' said Chick.

Colin helped him to some more pumpkin.

'What can I do to see Chloe again?' he said.

Chick looked at him and smiled.

'I can see I'm boring you stiff with my stories about Jean Pulse Heartre,' he said . . . 'I wish I *could* do something to help you. But what *can* I do? . . .'

'It's awful,' said Colin. 'I'm full of despair and yet, at the same time, I'm horribly happy. It's a nice kind of feeling to want something as badly as that.'

'I wish,' he went on, 'I were lying deep in lightly toasted grass, with sunshine and warm earth all around – the grass crisp and yellow as straw, you know what I mean, with hundreds of little buzzing insects, and clumps of soft dry moss too. One lies flat on one's tummy and stares. A hedge, some pebbles, a few gnarled trees and half-a-dozen leaves complete the scene. They're a great help.'

'And Chloe?' said Chick.

'And Chloe, of course,' said Colin. 'Chloe on my mind.'

They were quiet for a few moments. A bottle seized the opportunity presented by these moments to send out a crystalline sound that bounced backwards and forwards between the walls.

'Have some more wine,' said Colin.

'Yes,' said Chick. 'Thanks.'

Nicholas brought in the rest of the meal – pineapple shortbread with orange cream.

'Thank you, Nicholas,' said Colin. 'What would you do if you were me and you wanted to see a girl you were in love with again?'

'Good Lord, sir,' said Nicholas, 'I see what Mr Colin means . . . But I must confess, sir, that such a thing has never happened to me.'

'Of course,' said Chick. 'You're as tough as Tarzan. But everybody isn't like you!'

'Thank you for the compliment, sir. I'm very touched,' said Nicholas. 'If I were Mr Colin, sir,' he continued, addressing himself to Colin, 'then I would try – using as an agent the person at whose home I had met the person whose presence Mr Colin seems to be missing, sir – to gather what information I could concerning the habits and whereabouts of this said person.'

'Despite its convoluted phraseology, Nicholas,' said Colin, 'I think that your idea does indeed have possibilities. But you know how silly you are when you're in love. And that's why I didn't tell Chick that I'd thought of doing exactly what you've described a long time ago.'

Nicholas went back to the kitchen.

'He's priceless,' said Colin.

'Yes,' said Chick. 'He certainly knows how to cook.'

They drank some more wine. Nicholas came back with an enormous cake.

'Here's an extra dessert,' he said.

Colin picked up a knife, but held himself back just as he was going to cut the first slice.

'It's too beautiful to cut,' he said. 'Let's wait a moment.'

'Procrastination,' said Chick, 'is a prelude in a minor key.'

'What made you say that?' said Colin.

He took Chick's glass and filled it with golden wine that was as heavy as syrup but flowed like trampled ether.

'I don't know,' said Chick. 'It came without thinking.'

'Taste!' said Colin.

They both emptied their glasses.

'It's wild! . . .' said Chick, whose eyes began to glow and sparkle like traffic lights.

Colin put his hand on his heart.

'It's better than that,' he said. 'It's out of this world.'

'Of course,' said Chick. 'Because you're out of this world too.'

'I'm sure that if we drink enough,' said Colin, 'Chloe will walk in at any moment.'

'There's no proof!' said Chick.

'Are you daring me?' said Colin, holding out his glass.

Chick filled them both.

'Wait a moment!' said Colin.

He put out both the centre light and the little lamp on the table. The only light left in the room came from the green lamp shimmering over the Scottish ikon where Colin usually carried out his meditations.

'Oh . . .' gasped Chick.

In the crystal goblets the wine shone with a trembling phosphorescent glow which seemed to emanate from a myriad luminous spots of every colour beyond the rainbow.

'Drink up!' said Colin.

They drank. The sparkle stayed on their lips. Colin put on the lights again. He seemed to hesitate for a moment.

'We aren't going to make a habit of it,' he said, 'so let's finish the bottle.'

'How about cutting the cake?' said Chick.

Colin seized a silver knife and began to carve a spiral into the shiny white icing. He suddenly stopped and looked in surprise at what he had done.

'I'm going to try something,' he said.

He took a holly leaf from the sprig on the table. Holding the cake in one hand he began spinning it round quickly on the tip of his finger, and with the other hand he put one of the spikes of the holly into the groove.

'Listen! . . .' he said.

Chick listened. It was 'Chloe', in an arrangement by Duke Ellington.

Chick looked at Colin. He had turned very pale.

Chick took the knife from his hands and plunged it firmly into the cake. It split into two, and inside it there was a new article by Heartre for Chick, and a date with Chloe for Colin.

13

Colin stood on the corner of the square, waiting for Chloe. The square was perfectly round, with a circular church in the middle surrounded by pigeons, single flower-beds, double benches and, all round the edge, a stream of cars and buses. The sun too was waiting for Chloe, but it was passing the time while waiting in making shadows, germinating the seeds of wild oats in inconvenient cracks, flinging open shutters, pushing up blinds and making a lamppost, that was still alight because an elebeast had forgotten it, hang its head in shame.

Colin rolled back the tops of his gloves and rehearsed his first sentence. This grew quickly shorter and shorter as the moment drew nearer. He had no idea what he and Chloe were going to do. Maybe he could take her to a tea-shop, although he wasn't very fond of them. Middle-aged ladies gobbling cream cakes by the dozen with their little fingers sticking out always made him feel sad. He could only visualize stuffing as an honourable pastime for men as it took none of their natural dignity away from them. He couldn't take Chloe to the pictures – she would never agree to that. Nor to the Parliadium – she'd be bored. Nor to the human races – she'd be scared. Nor to the Cobblered Vic or the Old Witch – there's Noh playing there. Nor to the Mittish Bruiseum – there are wolves in their Assyrian folds. Nor to Whiskeyloo – there's not a single train there . . . only Pullman hearses.

'Hallo! . . .'

Chloe came up behind him. He quickly pulled off his glove, got tangled up with it inside out, punched himself on the nose, yelled 'Yowl' . . . and took her hand. She gave a tremendous smile.

'You're very clumsy! . . .'

A long-haired fur coat the same colour as her hair, a little fur hat, and Alice boots with fur tops.

She took Colin's arm.

'Let me take your arm. You seem a bit clueless today! . . .'

'Things did go better last time,' admitted Colin.

She laughed again, looked at him, and laughed even louder.

'You're laughing at me,' said Colin, crestfallen and feeling sorry for himself. 'It's not very kind of you.'

'Are you pleased to see me?' said Chloe.

'Oh, yes! Oh, yes! . . .' said Colin.

They started walking, letting the first pavement they came across guide their steps. A little pink cloud came down from the air and drew up close beside them.

'I'm going your way,' it winked.

'Let's step on then,' said Colin.

And the cloud wrapped itself round them. Inside the cloud it was warm, and it smelt of candy-floss and cinnamon.

'Nobody can see us any more! . . .' said Colin. 'But we can still see everything that is going on! . . .'

'I think it is slightly transparent,' said Chloe. 'Better be careful!'

'Who cares? And besides, it's much cosier,' said Colin. 'What would you like to do? . . .'

'Just walk . . . Would that bore you?'

'Not if you tell me stories . . .'

'I don't know any nice enough,' said Chloe. 'Let's see what's in the shop windows. Look at that! . . . Isn't it interesting . . .'

In the window a beautiful woman was lying on a spring mattress. Her breasts were exposed and an apparatus with fine white and long silky-haired brushes was steadily stroking them upwards. A notice at the side said *Save Shoe Leather With Reverend Charles's Antipodes*.

'What a good idea,' said Chloe.

'I don't get the connexion! . . .' said Colin. 'Anyway, it's much more fun to do it with your hands.'

Chloe blushed.

'Don't say things like that. I don't like boys who say naughty things to girls.'

'I'm awfully sorry . . .' said Colin. 'I didn't mean . . .'

He seemed so dejected that she smiled and nudged him playfully to show that she wasn't seriously angry.

In another window a fat man with a butcher's apron was cutting the throats of little children. It was a display advertising Family Allowances.

'So that's where all our money goes,' said Colin. 'It must cost a terrible lot to clear that up every evening.'

'They're not real! . . .' said Chloe, alarmed.

'How do you know?' said Colin. 'They get them for nothing on the National Assistance . . .'

'I don't like it,' said Chloe. 'We never used to have things like that in the shop windows. I don't think it's much of an improvement.'

'It doesn't matter,' said Colin. 'It only affects people who already believe in that stupid kind of thing . . .'

'And what's this? . . .' said Chloe.

In the next window was a fat round cherubic stomach sitting on a pair of rubber wheels. The notice read *Yours Won't Have Wrinkles Either If You Smooth It With An Electric Iron*.

'But I can recognize that! . . .' said Colin. 'It belongs to Serge, my old cook! . . . What's it doing there?'

'Don't start worrying about that,' said Chloe. 'I'm not going to let you find fault with that belly. It's far too fat, anyway . . .'

'That's because he was such a marvellous cook! . . .'

'Let's go somewhere else,' said Chloe. 'I don't want to do any more window-shopping. I don't like it so much now.'

'What shall we do then?' said Colin. 'Shall we have some tea somewhere?'

'Oh! . . . It isn't tea-time . . . Anyway, I prefer coffee.' Colin, relieved, took a deep breath, and his braces snapped.

'What was that funny noise?'

'I trod on a dead twig,' said Colin, blushing.

'How about a walk in the park?' said Chloe.

Colin looked at her, delighted.

'That's a marvellous idea. There won't be anyone about.'

This time Chloe blushed.

'That's not why I suggested it. Anyway,' she added as a form of revenge, 'we won't go off the pathways. We don't want to get our feet wet.'

He lightly increased the pressure on the arm he could feel beneath his own.

'Let's go through the subway,' he said.

The subway had rows of enormous aviaries on each side. This was where the Civic Controllers stored their spare pigeons for Public Squares and Monuments. There were also resting places for weary sparrows, nesting places for rearing sparrows, and testing places for cheering sparrows. People did not often stop in these parts because the wings of all those birds made a tremendous draught like a whirlwind full of whizzing blue and white feathers.

'Don't they ever sit still?' said Chloe, holding down her hat to prevent that flying away too.

'It isn't always like this,' said Colin.

He was struggling with the tail of his overcoat.

'Let's hurry and get past the pigeons – the sparrows don't create so much breeze,' said Chloe, pressing closer against Colin.

They hurried along and escaped from the danger zone. The little cloud had not followed them. It had taken a short cut and was sitting waiting for them at the other end.

14

The bench was dark green and felt slightly damp. Despite their fears the path was not a very busy one and they were snug and undisturbed there.

'You don't feel cold?' said Colin.

'No, not with this cloud round us,' said Chloe. 'But . . . I'd like to get even closer to you, all the same.'

'Oh! . . .' said Colin, and he blushed.

It gave him a strange sensation. He put his arm round Chloe's waist. Her hat was perched on the other side of her head and beneath his lips he had an ocean of lustrous hair.

'I like being with you,' he said.

Chloe said nothing. She breathed a little faster and by slow degrees drew imperceptibly closer to him.

Colin was whispering close into her ear.

'You're not bored?'

She shook her head, and Colin took advantage of this to move in still closer.

'I . . .' he said, as close to her ear as possible, and, at this very moment, as if by mistake, she turned her head and Colin found he was kissing her lips. It did not last very long; but the second time it was much, much better. Then he buried his face in her hair, and they stayed like that, without saying another word.

15

'It's nice of you to come, Alyssum,' said Colin. 'But you're going to be the only girl . . .'

'I don't mind,' said Alyssum. 'Chick's agreed.'

Chick nodded. But, to tell the truth, Alyssum's voice was not altogether gay.

'Chloe isn't in Paris,' said Colin. 'She's gone away for three weeks to see some relations in the country . . .'

'You must be feeling very lonely,' said Chick.

'I've never been happier in my life!' said Colin. 'I wanted to tell you that we've got engaged . . .'

'Congratulations!' said Chick, being careful not to look at Alyssum.

'What's the matter with you two?' said Colin. 'It looks as if something's wrong.'

'Nothing's the matter,' said Alyssum. 'It's only that Chick is so stupid.'

'I'm not,' said Chick. 'Don't take any notice of her, Colin . . . Nothing's wrong.'

'You're both saying the same thing, and yet you don't agree,' said Colin, 'therefore one of you – or both of you, perhaps – must be lying. Come on, the meal's ready. Let's go straight in and eat it.'

They went into the dining-room.

'Sit down, Alyssum,' said Colin. 'Sit down next to me and then you can tell me all your troubles.'

'Chick's stupid,' said Alyssum. 'He says it's wrong to keep me with him because he hasn't got the money to look after me properly, and yet he's ashamed of not marrying me.'

'I'm a bastard,' said Chick.

'I don't know what to say to you,' said Colin.

He was so happy that this grieved him more than it would have done at any other time.

'It certainly isn't the money,' said Chick. 'It's Alyssum's parents who don't want me to marry her – and they'll get their way. There's a story like that in one of Heartre's books.'

'It's a fabulous book,' said Alyssum. 'Have you read it, Colin?'

'Isn't that just like you!' said Colin. 'That's where the real trouble is. I'm sure all your money still goes on old Heartre.'

Chick and Alyssum let their noses dangle in shame.

'Only mine,' said Chick. 'Alyssum doesn't spend anything on Heartre any more. She hardly gives him a thought now that's she's living with me.'

There was a certain element of reproach in his tone.

'I like you better than Heartre,' said Alyssum.

She was nearly in tears.

'You're sweet,' said Chick, 'and I don't deserve you. But collecting Heartre is my only vice – and, as an engineer, unfortunately I can't afford to have more than one.'

'You're breaking my heart,' said Colin. 'Let's hope all your worries will sort themselves out. Undo your serviettes.'

Under Chick's there was a copy of *Vomition* bound in polecat and skunk, and under Alyssum's a wide gold ring in the shape of a nausea.

'Oh! . . .' gasped Alyssum.

She put her arms round Colin's neck and kissed him.

'You're a pal,' said Chick. 'I don't know how I can say thanks. Anyway, you know perfectly well that I can't possibly thank you in the way I'd like . . .'

Colin was beginning to feel slightly better. And Alyssum was really beautiful that evening.

'What perfume are you wearing?' he said. 'Chloe uses one made from essence of double-distilled orchids.'

'None at all,' said Alyssum.

'It's natural,' said Chick.

'It's terrific! . . .' said Colin. 'It's like the breeze in a forest – a forest filled with streams and squirrels and strange playful little animals.'

'Talk to us about Chloe! . . .' said Alyssum, flattered.

Nicholas brought in the hors d'oeuvres.

'Hallo, Nicholas,' said Alyssum. 'How are you?'

'Fine,' said Nicholas.

He put the plate on the table.

'Aren't you going to kiss me?' said Alyssum.

'Be my guest, Nicholas,' said Colin. 'You'd make me very happy if you'd come and have dinner with us . . .'

'Oh! Do . . .' said Alyssum. 'Come and eat with us.'

'Mr Colin plunges me into confusion, sir,' said Nicholas. 'I can hardly sit down at Mr Colin's table in these clothes . . .'

'Listen, Nicholas,' said Colin. 'Hurry off and change if you must – but I'm giving you orders to come and have dinner with us.'

'Thank you, Mr Colin, sir,' said Nicholas. 'I'll go and change then.'

He left the plate on the table and went out. 'Now,' said Alyssum, 'tell us about Chloe . . .'

'Help yourselves,' said Colin. 'I don't know what it is, but it's bound to be good.'

'Tell us about Chloe! . . .' screamed Chick. 'Our tongues are hanging out!'

'I'm going to marry Chloe in a month from today,' said Colin. 'And, oh, I wish it were going to be tomorrow! . . .'

'You're so lucky!' said Alyssum.

Colin felt happy that he was so rich.

'Listen, Chick,' he said. 'Would you like some of my money?'

Alyssum looked at Colin with great tenderness. He was so nice that you could see the blue and mauve thoughts running through the veins on the backs of his hands.

'I couldn't accept it,' said Chick.

'You'd be able to marry Alyssum,' said Colin.

'Her parents don't want us to,' replied Chick, 'and I don't want her to quarrel with them. Besides, she's too young . . .'

'I'm not as young as all that,' said Alyssum, suddenly sitting up straight on the quilted seat and bringing out the full value of her provocative breasts.

'That's not what he meant! . . .' interrupted Colin. 'Listen, Chick. I've got a hundred thousand doublezoons. I'll give you a quarter and then you'll be able to live in peace. You can carry on working – and like that, things should work out fine.'

'I'll never be able to thank you enough,' said Chick.

'Don't thank me,' said Colin. 'I'm not interested in the happiness of all men, but only in the happiness of each.' The door bell rang.

'I'll go and see who it is,' said Alyssum, 'I'm the youngest! Remember you were just complaining about it . . .'

She got up and her little feet skimmed the surface of the carpet.

It was Nicholas. He had gone down the fire escape and had come back dressed in a thick fawn and green sporran-spun herringbone tweed overcoat and a flat doughboy stetson. He had gloves of disinherited pigskin, and shoes made of solid snakeskin. When he took off his overcoat he appeared in all his splendour. His corduroy jacket was in rich chestnut with ivory furrows, and he wore it over esso-blue trousers with five-and-a-half-inch turnups.

'Oh!' said Alyssum. 'How smart you are! . . .'

'And how's my little niece? Just as lovely as ever? . . .' His hands roamed over her breasts and bottom.

'Come and sit down,' said Alyssum.

'Hallo, boys,' said Nicholas as he came in.

'At last!' said Colin. 'So you've finally decided to talk like everybody else!'

'Of course!' said Nicholas. 'I can do it when I want to. And while we're at it, shall we kick all the other formalities down the fire escape too? . . .'

'Of course,' said Colin. 'Sit down.'

Nicholas sat down facing Chick.

'Help yourself to hors d'oeuvres,' said Chick.

'Now,' said Colin, 'would you like to be my best man, Chick? And Nicholas, would you like to give Chloe away?'

'We'd love to,' beamed Nicholas. 'But don't try to match us up with any horrible bridesmaids. People are always trying to do that . . .'

'We're going to ask Alyssum and Isis to be bridesmaids,' said Colin, 'and the Kissitwell brothers to be fairies of honour.'

'Then it's all settled,' said Chick.

'Alyssum,' Nicholas went on, 'go to the kitchen and bring in the dish that's in the oven. It should be ready by now.'

She did as she was told and came back with a massive silver plate. And when Chick lifted the cover, they found underneath it two little figures carved from pâté de foie gras representing Colin in a top-hat and Chloe as a bride. All round the edge was written the date of the wedding and in a corner was the artist's signature – *Nicholas*.

16

Colin sprinted through the streets.

'It's going to be a lovely wedding . . . And it's tomorrow – tomorrow morning. And all my friends are going to be there . . .'

The street led straight to Chloe.

'Chloe, your lips are honey. Your complexion is peaches. Your eyes see things as we all should see them. Your body makes me feel warm . . .'

Glass marbles careered through the streets with children behind them.

'It will take months and months for your kisses to quench the thirst they have inspired in me. It will take years and years to extinguish the kisses I want to shower over you – on your hands, on your hair, on your eyes, on the nape of your neck . . .'

There were three little girls in the street. They were singing a very round round and dancing to it in a triangle.

'Chloe, I want to feel your breasts against my chest, with my two hands wrapped round you, your arms about my neck, your perfumed head in the hollow of my shoulder, and your palpitating skin and the scent of your body . . .'

The sky was blue and brilliant. The cold was still biting, but not quite so deeply. The trees, still deep black, displayed fat green buds at the tips of their lack-lustre limbs.

'When you are far from me, I see you in that dress with the silver buttons – but were you wearing it then? No, not the first time! You had it on the day we went out, under your soft heavy coat, but nothing under the dress . . .' He pushed open the shop door and went in. 'I'd like masses and masses of flowers for Chloe, please,' he said.

'When would you like them delivered?' asked the florist. She was a frail young girl with raw red hands. She loved flowers very much.

'Take them round tomorrow morning – and then bring some to me. I want our room to be full of white flowers – lilies, gladioli, roses and everything else that is white – and, right in the middle, an enormous bunch of red roses.'

17

The Kissitwell brothers were getting themselves ready for the wedding. They were often asked to be pansy page-boys because their appearance always added a fragrant charm to such occasions. They were twins. The name of the eldest was Coriolanus. He had wavy black hair, soft white skin, an air of virginity, the straightest of noses and blue eyes that sheltered behind heavy lids of creamy amber.

The youngest was called Pegasus, and looked very much like his brother, except that his eyelids were emerald green – and this was usually quite enough for people to tell one from the other. They had taken up homosexuality as a career because they had a vocation for it, and also because they needed the money. But, as they were being so well-paid for being pansy page-boys, they hardly worked seriously any more, and the noxious idleness that this thrust upon them drove them into the clutches of vice from time to time. And thus it was that, only yesterday, Coriolanus had behaved very naughtily with a little girl, Pegasus was lecturing him furiously, while massaging himself with rose-hip syrup (made from male bushes) in front of a big three-sided mirror.

'And what time did you get home last night, I'd like to know?' said Pegasus.

'I forget,' said Coriolanus. 'And don't stick your fat bottom into places that don't concern you!'

Coriolanus plucked at his eyebrows with pressurized tweezers.

'You're obscene!' said Pegasus. 'And with a girl too! . . . What would auntie say if she found out! . . .'

'Oh! . . . Haven't you ever stayed out late for a bit of fun then? Eh?' said Coriolanus, accusingly.

'When, I should like to know?' said Pegasus – the first signs of a little anxious frown beginning to appear all the same.

He stopped his auto-massage and began his slimming limbering-up exercises in front of the glass.

'All right,' said Coriolanus, 'I won't persecute you. I don't want to drive you back to where you came from. Come and zip up my pantees for me instead.'

They had specially made trousers with the flies up the back and they were difficult to do up alone.

'There!' sneered Pegasus, 'You see! You can't talk!'

'All right, that's enough!' repeated Coriolanus. 'Whose wedding are we going to today?'

'It's Colin marrying that Chloe,' said his brother disgustedly.

'Why d'you say it like that?' asked Coriolanus. 'He's a lovely boy.'

'Oh, yes, he's lovely all right,' said Pegasus, putting his tongue round his lips. 'But Chloe! She's got such round little titties that you could never take her for a boy! . . .'

Coriolanus blushed.

'Well I think she's sweet . . .' he murmured. 'She makes you feel you want to touch them . . . Doesn't she have that effect on you? . . .'

His brother looked at him, stupefied.

'You're a rotten pig!' he spluttered, using all his energy. 'You're the most depraved person I know . . . One of these days you'll end up marrying a woman! . . .'

18

Father Phigga came out of the undervestry, followed by his Unisexton Bedull and a Husher. They were carrying colossal corrugated cardboard cartons crammed with candles, coloured crepe and carnival decorations.

'When the Daubers' van comes, ask it to drive right up to the altar, Aubrey,' he said to the Husher.

This was because the majority of professional Hushers are called Marmaduke.

'And everything has got to be yellow?' said Aubrey.

'With purple stripes,' said the Unisexton Bedull. His name on the charts was Adam Browbeadle but he was really called Jeremiah Jingo. He was a big friendly rascal whose gold chain and uniform shone as brightly as a row of frozen noses.

'Yes,' said Father Phigga, 'because the Hamarishi Pibosh is coming on later in his caravan to give them the blessing. Come on, let's tart up the Minstrels' Gallery with the things in these boxes.'

'How many Minstrels are there?' asked the Husher.

'Three score and thirteen,' said the Unisexton Bedull.

'And twenty Twenty-Four-Sheet Music Boys,' said Father Phigga proudly.

The Husher gave a long low whistle.

'And only two people getting married!' he said with admiration.

'Yes,' said Father Phigga. 'That's the way rich folk do things.'

'And are there many people coming?' asked the Unisexton Bedull.

'Millions!' said the Husher. 'I'm going to carry my long red pikestaff and my big stick with the red knob.'

'Oh, no!' said Father Phigga. 'You ought to carry the yellow pikestaff and the purple stick – they're much more uppercrust, and you'll be as swish as a Swiss Guard.'

By now they were under the gallery. Father Phigga opened a little secret door in one of the supporting pillars. Like an Archimedean screw they began climbing up the narrow winding stair, one after the other. A vague glimmer of light came down on them from above.

After twenty-four turns of the screw they stopped for breath.

'It's hard work!' said Father Phigga.

The Husher, who was at the bottom, agreed, and Adam Browbeadle, who was in the middle, concurred with this observation.

'Only two more turns and a half,' said Father Phigga.

They emerged on to a platform at the opposite end of the church to the altar, a hundred yards up in the air, and the floor below could be barely seen through the mist. Clouds drifted into the church and floated across the nave in fat faithful flocks.

'It's going to be fine,' said the Unisexton Bedull, sniffing at the clouds. 'I can smell thyme passing.'

'There's hawthorn and catkin too,' said the Husher. 'I'm sure I got a whiff of them.'

'I hope the service will be a success!' said Father Phigga.

They put down their boxes and began to decorate the Minstrels' music-stands with chains and bells. The Husher unwrapped them, blew away the dust, and then passed them on to the Unisexton Bedull and Father Phigga.

Above them the pillars rose and rose and appeared to join together far, far away. The matt stone, a lovely creamy white in colour, was bathed in a calm, clear light reflected from the soft, sweet burst of day that caressed the church. At the very top everything was peacock-blue and turquoise.

'We'll have to polish up the mikes,' said Father Phigga to the Husher.

'I'm just unwinding my last chain!' said the Husher, 'then I'll get on with it.'

He took a red woollen duster out of his satchel and energetically began to rub the first microphone stand. There were four mikes, set out in a straight line at the front of the Minstrels' gallery and rigged up so that every time there was a peal of bells outside the church, a tune would be played inside.

'Hurry up, Aubrey,' said Father Phigga. 'Jeremiah and myself have finished.'

'Wait for me then,' said the Husher, 'I've got five minutes' grace.'

Adam Browbeadle and Father Phigga put the lids back on the boxes of decorations and stacked them in a corner of the gallery where they could easily be found again after the wedding.

'I'm ready,' said the Husher.

All three buckled the belts of their parachutes and leapt gracefully out into space. With a silky splash the three big rainbow-coloured flowers burst open and, some time later, they made perfect landings on the polished paving of the nave.

19

'Am I pretty?'

Chloe was looking at herself in the flecked silver bowl where an uninhibited goldfish was playfully performing. On her shoulder the grey mouse with the black whiskers scratched its nose with its paw and looked at the rippling reflections.

Chloe had put on her stockings – the same colour as her blonde skin, and as fine as the fumes of incense – and her high-heeled shoes of white leather. The rest of her was naked, except for a wide bangle of blue gold which made her delicate wrist seem even more slender.

'Do you think I should get dressed? . . .'

The mouse slid round Chloe's round neck and settled on one of her breasts. It looked up at her from below – and seemed to think that she should.

'In that case, I'll have to put you down!' said Chloe. 'You know you're going back to Colin's tonight. But don't forget to say good-bye to the others here! . . .'

She put the mouse down on the carpet, looked out of the window, let the curtain fall back and went over to her bed. Her white dress was all laid out on it, with Isis and Alyssum's water-clear dresses on either side.

'Are you two ready yet?'

In the bathroom, Alyssum was helping Isis do her hair. They too were already wearing their shoes and stockings.

'None of us is getting ready very quickly – either in there or out here,' said Chloe, pretending to be angry. 'Do you children realize that I'm getting married this morning?'

'You've still got a whole hour left!' said Alyssum.

'And that's plenty!' said Isis. 'Your hair's done already!' Chloe laughed, tossing her curls. It was warm in the steam-filled bathroom, and Alyssum's back was so appetizing that Chloe softly caressed it with the flat of her palms. Isis, sitting in front of the glass, let her supple scalp succumb to Alyssum's scientific manipulation.

'You're tickling!' said Alyssum, beginning to laugh.

Chloe touched her deliberately where she was most ticklish – under the arms right down to the hips. Alyssum's skin was warm and tingling.

'And what about me?' said Isis, who was doing her nails until they had finished.

'You're both so lovely,' said Chloe. 'It's a pity you can't come as you are. I wish you could both stay in just your shoes and stockings.'

'Go and get dressed, honey,' said Alyssum, 'or you'll miss everything.'

'Kiss me,' said Chloe. 'I'm so happy!'

Alyssum pushed her out of the bathroom and Chloe sat on the bed. She smiled to herself when she looked at the lace of her dress. First of all she put on a baby cellophane bra, and then a pair of white gingham pants. They brought out the beauty of her firm outlines to its fullest extent.

20

'All right?' said Colin.

'Not yet,' said Chick.

For the fourteenth time Chick was trying to tie Colin's tie and he just couldn't manage it.

'Try doing it with gloves on,' said Colin.

'Why?' asked Chick. 'Do you think it will work any better?'

'I don't know,' said Colin. 'It was just an idea.'

'A good job we gave ourselves plenty of time!' said Chick.

'Yes,' said Colin. 'But we'll still be late if we don't get this right.'

'Don't worry,' said Chick. 'We'll manage it soon.'

He performed a swift series of closely linked movements and sharply pulled both ends at the same time. The tie snapped in the middle and he was left holding half of it in each hand.

'That's number three!' remarked Colin. But his mind was elsewhere.

'All right,' said Chick, 'I know it is . . . Be patient!'

He sat down on a chair and thoughtfully rubbed his chin.

'I can't think what we're doing wrong,' he said.

'Neither can I,' said Colin. 'It's never happened before.'

'No,' said Chick, flatly. 'Let's try it without looking.'

He took a fourth tie and carelessly wound it round Colin's neck, while he let his eyes follow every detail of the flight of a flutterwing. He put the thick end over the thin one, brought it back through the loop, then with a twist to the right, a quick slip underneath, and . . . But unfortunately, at that very moment, his eyes fell on his work and both ends of the tie brutally snapped together, squashing his index finger. He yelped with pain.

'Oh, sod the existential horror!' he said.

'Did you hurt yourself?' asked Colin, full of sympathy. Chick was sucking his finger furiously.

'Now I'll have a black man's pinch,' he said.

'Poor old thing!' said Colin.

Chick muttered something and looked at Colin's neck.

'Just a minute! . . .' he whispered. 'It's tied itself. Don't move . . .'

He stepped back quietly, without lifting his eyes from the tie, and picked up a bottle of aerosol fixative from the table behind him. Slowly he steadied the extremity of the tiny tube as he took aim and stealthily closed in on the tie. Colin hummed quietly, pretending to be looking at the ceiling.

The fine spray landed bang on the heart of the knot. The tie sprang into the air, turned a rapid double somersault, and then fell rigidly into position, crucified by the solidifying spirit.

21

Colin left the house, followed by Chick. They were going to walk round to fetch Chloe. Nicholas was going straight to the church to join them there. He was putting the last touches to a special meal he was cooking that he had discovered in ffroydde and which ought to turn out terrifically.

There was a bookshop on the way and Chick stopped to look in the window. In the very centre of the display a copy of Heartre's *Mildew*, bound in purple morocco embossed with a clock standing at five o'clock to represent the arms of the Marchioness de Mauvoir, sparkled like a precious jewel.

'Oh!' said Chick. 'Just look at that! . . .'

'What?' said Colin, coming back. 'Oh! You mean that? . . .'

'Yes,' said Chick.

Just to look at the book made his mouth water. A narrow stream of saliva began to form on the pavement between his legs and wind its way down to the kerb, trickling round the little heaps of dirt.

'Well?' said Colin. 'You've already got it, haven't you? . . .'

'Not with a binding like that! . . .' said Chick. 'Oh, you're such a bore!' said Colin. 'Come on, we're supposed to be in a hurry.'

'I bet it's worth a doublezoon or two,' said Chick. 'Of course it is,' said Colin, and marched off. Chick went through his pockets. 'Colin!' he called . . . 'Lend me the money.' Colin stopped once again. He shook his head sadly. 'I don't think,' he said, 'that the twenty-five thousand doublezoons I promised you are going to last very long.'

Chick blushed, his nose drooped, but nevertheless he still held out his hand. He took the cash and sped into the shop. Colin waited outside, anxiously and impatiently. Seeing Chick come out with such a radiant smile he shook his head once again, in pity this time, and a semi-smile sketched itself across his own lips.

'You're nuts, my poor Chick! How much was it?' 'Forget it,' said Chick. 'Come on, let's run.' They hurried off. Chick seemed to be galloping on seven-league dragons.

Outside Chloe's door people were admiring the handsome white car ordered by Colin that had just driven up with its liveried chauffeur. The seats were covered in white fur, and inside it was all warm and cosy and full of music.

The colour of the sky was permanent blue and the clouds

were scarce and wispy. It wasn't too cold. The winter was coming to an end.

The bottom of the lift began to swell under their feet and, with a big soft huff and a puff, gently burst its way up to the right floor, carrying them with it. Its door glided open for them. They rang. Then the flat door opened. Chloe was waiting for them.

Besides her cellophane bra, her little white pants and her stockings, her body was protected by two layers of muslin, with a very full veil of fine tulle that fell from her shoulders, leaving her head completely free.

Alyssum and Isis were dressed in the same way, but their dresses were the colour of water. Their perfumed hair shone in the sunshine and the heavy locks nestled lightly on their shoulders. A choice between them would have been impossible. Colin knew how to make it. He dared not kiss Chloe for fear of spoiling the way she had been arranged, so he made up for it with Isis and Alyssum. They were more than willing to help him out, seeing how happy he was.

The whole room was filled with white flowers – the ones Colin had chosen – and on the pillow of the unmade bed there was the single petal of a crimson rose. The smell of the flowers and the perfume of the girls mingled intimately and Chick took himself for a bee in a hive. Alyssum wore a lilac orchid in her hair, Isis a scarlet rose and Chloe a big white camellia. She held a spray of lilies and a tiny chain of ivy leaves, all freshly lacquered and glistening, shone beside her wide bracelet of blue gold. Her engagement ring was inset with little square and rectangular diamonds which spelt out the name *Colin* in Morse. Under a vase of flowers in a corner, the summit of a cameraman's skull slowly rose. He was shooting among the leaves down below.

Colin posed for a few moments with Chloe, and then with Chick, Alyssum and Isis. Then they all lined up and followed Chloe into the lift. Its cables stretched so much under the extra weight that there was no need to press the button – but they all took great care to jump off at the same time so that there would be no chance of any of them being swept up again with the car.

The chauffeur opened the door. The three girls and Colin sat in the back, with Chick in the front – and off they went. All the people in the street looked round and energetically waved, thinking it was Royalty or the President, and then went on their way, filled with shining golden thoughts.

The church was not far away. The car whizzed round elegantly in the shape of a heart and pulled up at the foot of the steps.

At the top of them, between two big pillars covered with carving, Father Phigga, the Unisexton Bedull and the Husher were on parade prior to the ceremony. As a backcloth, long lengths of white silk hung to the ground, and the twenty Twenty-Four-Sheet Music Boys were dancing a ballet. They were wearing white cassocks, with red shorts and white shoes. The girls, who had been called in to make up the right number and to make things more pleasant, wore little red pleated mini-skirts instead of the shorts, and had red feathers in their hair. Father Phigga was on the drums, the Unisexton Bedull on the fife, and the Husher backed them up with maracas. All three joined in the chorus together, after which Father Phigga did a quick dance, then grabbed a double-bass and with his bow gave a fabulous solo based on variations on the main theme from the Bridal March.

The three score and thirteen Minstrels were already up in their gallery playing, and the bells were ringing merrily on high.

Suddenly a brutally discordant and hopelessly lost chord rang out. The conductor, who had taken a step back too near the edge, had just toppled over into space, and the deputy conductor had to take over without a break. At the very moment that the first conductor squashed himself flat on the floor-slabs below, they played another shattering chord to cover the din, although the church still trembled on its foundations.

Colin and Chloe looked with admiration at Father Phigga, the Unisexton Bedull, the Husher and his Hush-Hushers and Offsidesmen as they stood to attention at the door of the church waiting for the ceremony of the presentation of the pikestaff.

As a finale, Father Phigga did a juggling turn with chopsticks and Indian clubs, and Adam Browbeadle produced such an agonized caterwauling from his fife that half the narrow-minded old maids who had been waiting on the steps to see the bride forced a straight and narrow path through the crowd to scurry inside and pray. On the last chord the Husher snapped the strings of his double-bass. Then the twenty Twenty-Four-Sheet Music Boys came down the steps, one after the other, with the girls forming up on the right, and the boys on the left, of the door of the car.

Chloe stepped out. She was completely radiant and ravishing in her white dress. Alyssum and Isis followed her. Nicholas had just arrived and hurried to join the group. Colin took Chloe's arm, Nicholas took Isis's, and Chick took Alyssum's, and they all mounted the steps, followed by the Kissitwell brothers – Coriolanus on the right and Pegasus on the left – while the twenty Twenty-Four-Sheet Music Boys trotted along behind in twos. Father Phigga, the Unisexton Bedull and the Husher, after they had put down their instruments, held hands and danced in a ring while they waited.

Half-way up the steps, Colin and his friends carried out a complicated manoeuvre in which they all changed places and got themselves in the right order for going into church. Colin was with Alyssum, Nicholas with Chloe on his arm, followed by Chick and Isis and, last of all, the Kissitwell brothers – but this time with Pegasus on the right and Coriolanus on the left. Father Phigga and his stony henchmen stopped going round in circles, went to the head of the procession and then, singing a gay old Gregorian chant, made a dash for the door. As they passed through, the Hush-Hushers banged each of them on the head with a thin crystal balloon filled with consecrated water, and stuck a little stick of lighted incense in their hair. It burned with a yellow flame for the men and a purple one for the remaining sex.

The little trucks were all lined up inside the door of the church. Colin and Alyssum got into the first one and went straight off. They immediately found they were in a shadowy vaulted tunnel smelling of religion. The truck thundered along the track like lightning, and echoing music skidded along behind them. At the end of the tunnel the truck pushed through a pair of doors, turned sharply, and Saint Roland o' the Kirk appeared in a green spotlight. He stuck out his tongue at them, and Alyssum clung tightly to Colin. Spiders' webs swept across their cheeks, and fragments of prayers sprang into their minds. The second vision showed the Virgin and the third was God himself, who had a black eye and looked horribly grim and grumpy. Colin managed to remember a whole prayer and quickly whispered the words to Alyssum . . .

The truck came out under the dome with a deafening crash and stopped dead. Colin got out, let Alyssum go to her seat and then waited for Chloe who emerged soon after them.

They looked at the inside of the church. An enormous crowd of people was there. Everybody they knew had come. They were all listening to the music and making the most of the splendour and fun.

The Husher and Adam Browbeadle, leapfrogging about in their best robes, appeared heralding Father Phigga who had the Hamarishi Pibosh on his arm. Everybody stood up, and the Hamarishi Pibosh sat down in a big velvet chair. The noise of the other chairs scraping on the floor tiles was very harmonious.

The music came to a sudden stop. Father Phigga knelt down before the altar, banged his head three times on the carpet, and the Unisexton Bedull went down to lead Colin and Chloe to their places while the Husher was arranging the Twenty-Four-Sheet Music Boys on each side of the altar. By now a profound silence had filled the church and everybody was holding their breath.

Great rays of light were shining everywhere, trying to pick out anything golden so that they could burst out again into every direction. The wide yellow and purple painted stripes made the nave of the church look like the abdomen of an enormous sleeping wasp – seen from the inside.

Very high up the Minstrels began to hum a distant chorus. The clouds came in to listen. They smelt of coriander and mountain grass. It was warm in the church and the audience felt as if it were wrapped in an atmosphere of gracious cotton-wool.

Kneeling before the altar on a pair of inflated prayer-cushions covered in white velvet, Colin and Chloe, hand in hand, were waiting. Father Phigga was quickly flicking through a big book in front of them because he couldn't remember the recipe. From time to time he would throw a glance at Chloe because he was very taken by her dress. At last he stopped turning the pages, lifted his head, made a sign to the conductor with his hand, and the orchestra attacked the overture.

Father Phigga took a deep breath and began to sing, supported by a backing of eleven baffled trumpets playing in unison. The Hamarishi Pibosh was quietly dozing, his hand on his cross-bucolic. He knew that they would wake him up when it was his turn to sing.

The overture and prelude were written on old classic blues themes. For the anthem, Colin had asked them to play an arrangement by Duke Ellington of a popular old song, 'Chloe'.

Over the rail, beyond Colin, you could see Jesus on his big black cross. He seemed pleased that he had been invited and was watching everything with keen interest. Colin was holding Chloe's hand and smiled shyly up at Jesus. He began to feel a little tired. The service had cost him quite a lot – five thousand doublezoons – but he was happy because it had all turned out so well.

There were flowers all round the altar. And he was very fond of the music they were playing at that moment. He looked at Father Phigga and let him see that he had recognized the tune. Then he let his eyes close gently, leaned forward very slightly, and said 'I will'.

Chloe said 'I will' too, and Father Phigga shook both their hands with great vigour. The orchestra struck up again louder than ever, and the Hamarishi Pibosh got up to make the sermon in his ebony diction. The Husher hurriedly slipped between two rows of the congregation to bring his cane down smartly on Chick's fingers because he was looking at his new book instead of paying attention.

22

The Hamarishi Pibosh had gone. Colin and Chloe were in the undervestry collecting all the handshakes that their friends were giving them to bring them luck. Some people brought them useful tips for the night, and a passing pedlar suggested they might like some helpfully instructive photos. They began to feel very weary. The music was still playing and people were dancing in the church where they were serving holy ices and pious refreshments with little codfish sandwiches. Father Phigga had got back into his everyday clothes with a big hole in the seat of his pants – but he was looking forward to buying himself a new outfit out of the five thousand doublezoons. Moreover, he had just swindled the band in the traditional manner by refusing to pay for the conductor's name since he had pancaked out before the start of the service. Adam Browbeadle and the Husher were undressing the Twenty-Four-Sheet Music Boys and folding up their fancy costumes. The Husher was making a special fuss of the little girls. The Hush-Hushers and Offsidesmen, taken on as extras, had scooted. The Daubers' van was waiting outside. They were getting ready to scrub off the yellow and purple stripes and put them back into horrible caked-up old tins.

Standing on each side of Colin and Chloe, Alyssum and Chick and Isis and Nicholas were also making a collection of handshakes. The Kissitwell brothers were just handing in theirs. When Pegasus saw his brother getting too close to Isis, he pinched his bottom as viciously as he could, yelling out at the same time about what a terrible pervert he was.

There were still a dozen people left. They were Colin and Chloe's very special friends who were going to the wedding reception and feast. They all left the church, taking one last look at the flowers on the altar. The cold air hit them when they reached the steps outside. Chloe began to cough and hurried down the steps into the warm waiting car. She huddled up into the cushions and waited for Colin.

The others stood on the steps and watched the Minstrels go off – because they were all badly in debt they were being taken away in a black van, whose hooter played the tune 'Maria'. They were squeezed up inside it as tightly as a bunch of asparagus so, to get their own back, they all blew into their instruments which, when the fiddlers did it, made the most abominable din that had ever been heard in the district.

23

Colin's bedroom was a perfect cube in shape, which made the ceiling seem fairly lofty. The daylight came in through a window two feet high which ran all the way round the walls at a height of about four feet ten from the floor. The floor had thick burnt-orange close-carpeting, and the walls were hung with natural leather.

The bed did not stand on the floor, but was on a projecting platform half-way up the wall. It was reached by means of a little ladder of perfumigated oak with satin bronze and organza aluminium fittings. The space under the platform with the bed on it became the dressing-room. There were bookshelves in it, some comfortable armchairs and a photo of the Dalai-Lama.

Colin was still asleep. Chloe had just woken up and was looking down at him. Her hair was dishevelled and she looked even younger that way. There was only one sheet left on the bed – the one underneath them. The rest had flown all round the room – which was heated by currents of warm air. She was sitting now, her knees drawn up to her chin, rubbing her eyes – then she stretched out and let herself fall back. The pillow curved gently under the charming weight of her head.

Colin was flat on his belly, cuddling the bolster and drooling like a big baroque cherub. Chloe started laughing and knelt down beside him to give him a vigorous shake. He woke up, raised himself on his wrists, sat up and kissed her before he opened his eyes. Chloe allowed him to do all this without objecting, carefully guiding him to all the best places. Her golden skin was as soft and sweet as marzipan.

The grey mouse with the black whiskers climbed all the way up the ladder and came to tell them that Nicholas was waiting. They remembered they were going on their honeymoon and leapt out of bed. When the mouse realized that they weren't looking, it delved deeply into a giant box of sapodilla goodies that was at the side of the bed.

They washed themselves very quickly, put on matching

outfits and hurried to the kitchen. Nicholas had asked them to take breakfast in his kingdom. The mouse followed them, but stopped in the corridor. It wanted to find out why the suns weren't coming through as brilliantly as usual, and give them a good telling-off when they did.

'Well,' said Nicholas, 'did you sleep well?'

Nicholas's eyes had dark rings round them and the rest of his complexion matched.

'Marvellously,' said Chloe, letting herself sink on to a chair as she was finding it hard to stay standing.

'How about you?' asked Colin, who stumbled and picked himself up again once he was sitting on the floor, having made no effort to catch himself on the way down.

'I took Isis back home,' said Nicholas, 'and she gave me a drink like a good girl should.'

'Weren't her parents there?' asked Chloe.

'No,' said Nicholas, 'just her two little cousins, and they absolutely insisted that I should stay.'

'How old were they?' asked Colin insidiously.

'I don't know,' said Nicholas, 'but from the feel of them, I'd say that one was about sixteen and the other eighteen.'

'Did you spend the whole night there?' asked Colin.

'Hrmm! . . .' said Nicholas . . . 'All three of them were a little bit squiffy, so . . . so I had to put them all to bed. Isis's bed is very wide – the kind where there is always room for one more. I didn't want to disturb you, so I slept with them.'

'Slept? . . .' said Chloe . . . 'The bed may have been wide, but it must have been very hard because you don't look as if you got much rest.'

Nicholas gave a very unnatural little cough and started fiddling with his electrical gadgets.

'Taste this,' he said, trying to change the subject.

It was some apricots stuffed with dates and figs in an unctuous syrup that was candied on top.

'Will you be all right for driving?' asked Colin.

'I'll do my best,' said Nicholas.

'This is scrumptious,' said Chloe. 'Do bring some with us, Nicholas.'

'I'd prefer something more fortifying,' he replied.

And under the eyes of Colin and Chloe he concocted a revolting brew for himself. Into a glass of white wine he mixed a spoonful of vinegar, the yolks of five eggs, two oysters, four ounces of raw minced meat, some fresh cream and a pinch of bicarbonate of soda. The whole lot slipped down his gullet with a noise like a cyclotron doing a ton.

'Well?' said Colin, who had almost split his sides laughing when he saw the face Nicholas was pulling.

'That's better . . .' replied Nicholas, after a tremendous gulp.

Indeed, the bags under his eyes shrivelled up as if they had been smoothed away with benzine, and his whole complexion seemed to take on a new brilliance and glow. He shook his feathers up, clenched his fists, and roared. Chloe looked at him, slightly worried.

'You haven't got stomach-ache, Nicholas?'

'Of course not! . . .' he bellowed. 'It's all gone. You drink the rest – and then we'll set off.'

24

The big white car carefully carved its way over the lumps and bumps and through the ruts and furrows of the groovy road. Colin and Chloe, sitting at the back, looked sadly and soulfully at the passing landscape. The sky was overcast. Red birds flew as low as the telegraph wires, going up and down with the same monotonous rhythm, and their harsh piercing shrieks echoed back from the leaden water of the long never-ending puddles.

'Why are we coming this way?' Chloe asked Colin.

'It's a short cut,' said Colin. 'But you are forced to take it. The main road is worn out. Everyone kept on using it because the weather was always fine there – and now there's only this road left. Don't worry. Nicholas is a very good driver.'

'It's this unusual light,' said Chloe.

Her heart was beating fast, as if it had been squeezed inside a stiff, crusty shell. Colin put his arm round Chloe and, slipping his hand under her hair, playfully pinched the back of her graceful neck as if he were picking up a little kitten.

'Oh . . .' said Chloe, letting her head sink into her shoulders while Colin tickled her. 'Hold me close . . . I'm so scared when I'm all alone . . .'

'Would you like the yellow windows?' said Colin.

'I'd like all the colours . . .'

Colin pressed green, blue, yellow and red buttons and a succession of correspondingly coloured panes appeared in place of the plain ones round the car. It was like being on the inside of a rainbow, and striped shadows danced over the white fur between each telegraph pole. Chloe began to feel better.

Sparse and faded green moss ran along both sides of the road and, every now and again, there was a gnarled gesticulating tree. Not a breath of wind rumpled the cloaks of mud which squelched under the wheel of the car. Nicholas worked hard to keep the car under control and struggled to make it stick to the middle of the subsiding roadway.

He looked round for a second.

'Don't worry,' he said to Chloe, 'it won't be like this for long. The road gets better soon.'

Chloe looked out of the window by her side and shuddered. A squamaceous monster was standing beside a telegraph pole staring at them.

'Colin, look! . . . What's that?'

'I don't know,' he said. 'But I don't think it's dangerous . . .'

'It's only a man repairing the telegraph wires,' Nicholas called over his shoulder. 'They're dressed like that so that they don't get all muddy inside . . .'

'But it . . . it was horribly ugly . . .' murmured Chloe.

Colin kissed her.

'Don't be scared, Chloe dear, it was only a man . . .'

The road began to feel firmer under the wheels of the car. A glimmer of light tinted the horizon.

'Look,' said Colin. 'The sun is rising . . .'

Nicholas shook his head to show that he was wrong.

'It's the copper mines,' he said. 'We've got to go through them.'

The mouse, sitting by the side of Nicholas, cocked up an ear.

'It's true, I'm afraid,' said Nicholas. 'But it will be warmer there.'

The road took several more turns. Now steam began to

rise from the mud. The car was surrounded by white clouds with a strong smell of copper. Then the mud became completely solid and the old road emerged, cracked and dusty. Far ahead the air was trembling as if it were hovering over a great furnace.

'I don't like it,' said Chloe. 'Can't we go another way?'

'It's the only way,' said Colin. 'Would you like to look at the Cookery Book? . . . I've brought it with us . . .'

They had brought no other luggage, counting on buying everything on the way.

'Shall I lower the coloured windows?' asked Colin again.

'Please,' said Chloe. 'The light isn't so bad now.'

The road twisted again sharply, and they were suddenly in the midst of the copper mines. The mines went down on each side in steps, a few yards at a time. Enormous deserts of arid greenish copper unrolled out into infinity. Hundreds of men, dressed in goggled dungarees, were moving around in the flames. Others were stacking up the fuel in regular geometric pyramids. Electric trucks were continuously bringing more. Under the effects of the heat, the copper melted and ran in red streams fringed with spongy slag that was as hard as stone. At certain spots it was directed off into great reservoirs where pumps poured it into oval pipes.

'What a terrible job! . . .' said Chloe.

'They're very well paid,' said Nicholas.

Some of the men stopped to watch the car go past. The only thing that could be seen in their eyes was a look of lightly mocking pity. They were big and strong, and they looked as if nothing could harm them.

'They don't like us,' said Chloe. 'Let's go away.'

'It's because they're working . . .' said Colin.

'That's not a reason,' said Chloe.

Nicholas put his foot on the accelerator. The car whizzed over the frowning road, breaking through the barrier of noise from the machines and the smelting copper. 'We'll soon be on the old road again,' said Nicholas.

25

'Why were they so scornful?' asked Chloe. 'Work isn't so wonderful . . .'

'They've been told that it is,' said Colin. 'And lots of people do believe that it's good. But nobody really thinks it is. They do it out of habit and precisely in order not to have to think about it.'

'At any rate, it's stupid to do work that machines could do just as well.'

'Those machines have still got to be made . . .' said Colin. 'And who's going to do that?'

'Mm . . . Of course,' said Chloe. 'If you want an egg, you need a chicken – but once you've got a chicken you can have millions of eggs. So it's best to begin with the chicken.'

'What we need to find out,' said Colin, 'is who it is that stops people making such machines. They must need more time. People waste their time living, so that there's none left over for them to work in.'

'You mean the other way round, don't you?' said Chloe.

'No,' said Colin. 'If they had time to make the machines, they wouldn't need to do anything afterwards. What I mean is that they work in order to live instead of working in order to make machines which would let them live without having to work.'

'It's a bit complicated . . .' was Chloe's verdict on that.

'No,' said Colin, 'it's very simple. Of course, it would have to be done by degrees. But people waste so much time making things that wear out . . .'

'But don't you think they'd rather stay at home kissing their wives and going swimming and to the pictures? . . .'

'No,' said Colin, 'I don't. But only because they don't think so themselves.'

'But it's not their fault if they think work is so terrific, is it?'

'No,' said Colin, 'it's not their fault. It's because they've been taught that "Work is holy, good and beautiful. It counts above everything else, and the workers alone will inherit the earth". Only things have been arranged so that they have to spend all their time working and there's no time left for the rest of it to come true.'

'Well, they must be stupid then!' said Chloe.

'Yes, of course they're stupid,' said Colin. 'That's why they agree with those people who want them to think that work is the best possible thing for them. It stops them thinking for themselves and trying to reach a state where they wouldn't need to work any more.'

'Let's talk about something else,' said Chloe. 'Things like that are so dull. Tell me you like my hair . . .'

'I've already said that I do . . .'

He lifted her up and put her on his knees. Once again he felt completely happy.

'I've already told you that I love you enormously – the whole of you and every little particle and detail . . .'

'Well then, start going into details,' said Chloe, letting herself sink into Colin's arms as cuddly as a contented cobra.

26

'Excuse me sir,' said Nicholas. 'But would Mr Colin like us to stop here?'

The car had stopped at the side of the road in front of a hotel. This was the right road, solid and smooth, rippling with photogenic reflections, with perfectly cylindrical trees on both sides, lush green grass, sunshine, cows in meadows, worm-eaten fences, flowering hedgerows, orchards with apples on the trees, little mounds of autumn leaves and scattered drifts of snow here and there to prevent the landscape from becoming monotonous. There were palm-trees, mimosa and Northern pines in the garden of the hotel, and a redheaded, tousle-haired boy chasing two sheep and a drunken dog. On one side of the road the wind was blowing, and on the other it was not. You could take your choice of which side you liked best. Every other tree gave shade, and in the ditch on one side only could there be found frogs.

'Yes, let's stop here,' said Colin. 'We won't get to the sea today, anyway.'

Nicholas opened the door and jumped out. He was wearing a splendid chauffeur's uniform of pigskin with a very slick cap to match. He took two steps back and surveyed the car. Colin and Chloe got out too.

'Our conveyance is considerably soiled, sir,' said Nicholas. 'It's all that mud we've been through.'

'It doesn't matter,' said Chloe. 'They'll give it a wash at the hotel.'

'Go in and see if they've got any rooms for us,' said Colin, 'and anything nutritious we can eat.'

'Very good, sir,' said Nicholas, smartly bringing his hand up to his cap in a more exasperating manner than ever.

The velvet-covered rail on the polished oak gates in the fence sent shivers of delight running up his spine as he put his hand on it. His footsteps crunched over the gravel path, and he went up the two steps. The glazed door gave way as he pushed it and he disappeared inside the building.

The blinds were down and it was all very quiet. The sun was gently baking the windfalls and hatching them out into fresh little green apple-trees which instantly burst into blossom and gave even smaller apples. By the third generation all that could be seen was a kind of pink and green froth in which minute apples rolled around like marbles.

A few animals were snoozing in the sun, carrying out certain of their duties by spinning time on the spot. On the windy side of the road the graminivorous ones were slyly tucking in, and rotating leaves and feathers flew with a sound like crumpled silver paper. Some sharded insects tried to fight against the current, producing a soft splashing sound like the wheels of a paddle-steamer lashing into a great lake.

Colin and Chloe, in each other's arms, bathed in the sunshine, not saying a word, although their hearts were beating together to a boogie rhythm.

The glass door gave a little squeak. Nicholas was standing there again. His cap was on sideways and his suit was rumpled with all the buttons in the wrong holes.

'Have they kicked you out?' asked Colin.

'No, sir,' said Nicholas. 'They will be pleased to accept Mr Colin and his wife – and they can service the car too.'

'But whatever happened to you?' asked Chloe.

'Hrrm! . . .' said Nicholas. 'The manager isn't there . . . so his daughter saw to me instead . . .'

'Put yourself straight,' said Colin. 'You're indecent.'

'I should be grateful if Mr Colin would forgive me, sir,'

said Nicholas, 'but I thought that the two rooms were worth a little sacrifice . . .'

'Go and put your civilian clothes on,' said Colin, 'and start speaking normally. You're beginning to drive me round the bend! . . .'

Chloe stopped to play with a little mound of snow.

The flakes, soft and cool, did not melt and stayed perfectly white.

'Look how pretty it is,' she said to Colin.

Underneath the snow there were primroses, cornflowers and poppies.

'Yes,' said Colin. 'But you shouldn't play with it. You'll get cold.'

'I shan't!' said Chloe, and her cough was like a rip through a gorgeous piece of wild silk.

'Chloe dear,' said Colin, putting his arm round her, 'don't cough like that. I can't bear it!'

She left the snow which was slowly falling like baby feathers and began to glow again in the sun.

'I don't like that snow,' murmured Nicholas.

He remembered himself immediately.

'I beg Mr Colin to forgive my freedom of expression, sir.'

Colin pulled off one of his shoes and flung it straight at Nicholas's head. Nicholas was just bending down to scrape a minute stain off his trousers and stood up in surprise to see what had happened when he heard the window crash.

'Oh, sir! . . .' said Nicholas, full of reproach. 'That's Mr Colin's bedroom window!'

'Just too bad!' said Colin. 'Now we'll have a bit of fresh air . . . And that will teach you not to talk like an automatic idiot . . .'

He hopped through the hotel door, helped by Chloe.

The window-pane was beginning to grow again. A thin opalescent skin was forming on the edges of the frame, shimmering and iridescent with flashes of vague mysterious colours that were constantly changing.

27

'How did you sleep?' asked Colin.

'Not too badly. How about you?' said Nicholas, like a normal human being this time.

Chloe yawned and reached for the jug of black bean-syrup.

'That broken window stopped me sleeping,' she said.

'Hasn't it healed up yet?' asked Nicholas.

'Not altogether,' said Chloe. 'The trephination is still wide enough to let a piercing draught come through. This morning there was a flurry of snow all over my chest . . .'

'It's murder,' said Nicholas. 'I'll give them a piece of my mind. By the way, are we off again this morning?'

'This afternoon,' said Colin.

'I'm afraid I'll have to put on my chauffeur's uniform,' said Nicholas.

'Oh! Nicholas . . .' said Colin, 'if you start that again . . . I'll . . .'

'Yes,' said Nicholas, 'but there's no need to now.'

He swallowed his bowl of black bean-syrup and finished his bread and butter.

'I'll go and take a look at the kitchen,' he announced, getting up and straightening his tie with a pocket brace-and-bit.

He left the room and the sound of his steps could be heard getting fainter and fainter as they drew nearer to what was in all probability the kitchen.

'What would you like us to do today, Chloe?' asked Colin.

'I'd like you to kiss me, and me to kiss you,' said Chloe.

'Sure! . . .' replied Colin. 'And then what?'

'And then . . .' said Chloe, '. . . but I can't say it out loud . . .'

'Fine,' said Colin, 'but after that?'

'After that,' said Chloe, 'it will be lunchtime. Hold me in your arms. I'm cold. It's that snow . . .'

Sunshine floated into the room on golden waves.

'It's not cold here,' said Colin.

'No,' said Chloe, snuggling up to him, 'but I am. And afterwards I'll drop a line to Alyssum . . .'

28

Right from the start of the street the crowd were pushing and shoving to get into the hall where Jean Pulse Heartre was going to give his lecture.

People were using all kinds of tricks to needle through the eagle eye of the chastity belt of special duty policemen who had cordoned off the district and who were there to examine every invitation card and ticket, because hundreds and thousands of forgeries were in circulation.

One group drew up in a hearse and the coppers stuck a long steel spike through the coffin, crucifying the occupants to the elm for eternity. This saved having to take them out again before the funeral and the only trouble caused was that the shrouds would be all messy when the real dead men came to use them. Others got themselves parachuted in by special plane. There were riots and fighting too at Orly to get on to the planes. A team of firemen took them for a practice target and, unlacing their hoses, squirted them straight in the bulls-eye of the battle where everybody was miserably drowned. Others, in a desperate attempt, were trying to get in through the sewers. They were being pushed down again by hob-nailed boots which jumped heavily on their knuckles every time they tried to get a hold by gripping the edges of the man-holes. The sewer rats took over from there. But nothing could dampen the spirits of these aficionados. They weren't the same, however, as the ones who were drowning and who continued to struggle, the sounds of their efforts rising up to heaven and bouncing back off the clouds with a cavernous rumbling.

Only the pure, the really turned-on group, the intimate friends, had genuine tickets and invitation cards which could be very easily picked out from the forgeries. For this reason they slipped in unhindered between the buildings along a narrow alley which was protected every eighteen inches by a secret agent disguised as a Turkish Delight or a Mud Guard. Even so, there was still a tremendous number of genuine ticket-holders, and the hall, which was already brim-full, continued to welcome new arrivals every minute.

Chick had been there since the day before. For gold he had obtained from the doorman the right to take his place and, in order to make such a switch-over plausible, had broken the left leg of the said doorman with a surplus second-hand crowbar. There was no question of sparing his doublezoons where Heartre was concerned. Alyssum and Isis sat with him, waiting for the speaker to arrive.

They had spent the night there too, anxious not to miss the great occasion. Chick, in his Sherwood green attendant's uniform, looked as sexy as a dream. He had neglected his work badly since he had come into possession of Colin's twenty-five thousand doublezoons.

The scampering, scurrying public was made up of some very odd types. There were bespectacled pyramidal faces with lapel-length hair, yellow dog-ends and unshaven pimples, and girls with scruffy little plaits wound round and round their skulls, and lumber-doublets worn next to the skin with Elizabethan slashings giving shadowy vistas on to moony crescents of sliced breast.

In the great hall on the ground floor, with its half-glazed ceiling half-decorated with heavy water-colours, ideal for giving birth to doubts in the minds of the audience about the fun of an existence peopled with such off-putting feminine forms, more and more people were gathering, and latecomers found they had to resort to standing on one foot at the back – the other being required to kick away any neighbours who got too close. All eyes in the cadaverous crowd were on the special box in which the Marchioness de Mauvoir sat on a throne with her retainers, insulting the temporary nature of the seating arrangements of a row of philosophers, who were perched on gallery stools, by the old-fashioned luxury of her noble elevated position.

It was almost time for the lecture, and the crowd was growing hectic. An organized din came from the back of the hall, set up by several students trying to sow seeds of revolt in the spirits of the faithful by declaiming aloud passages selected at random from *The Bourbon on The Bounce* by Baroness Orczy.

But Jean Pulse was drawing near. The sounds of an

elephant's trunk could be heard in the street, and Chick leaned out of his box-office window. In the far distance the silhouette of Jean Pulse emerged from an armoured howdah, under which the rough and wrinkled hide of the elephant took on a bizarre appearance in the glow of a red headlamp. At each corner of the howdah a hand-picked marksman, armed with an axe, stood at the ready. The elephant was striding its way through the crowd, and the fearsome plod of the four columns moving through the crushed bodies unrelentingly drew on. At the main gate the elephant knelt down and the specially selected marks-men got off. With a graceful leap, Heartre landed in their midst and, hacking out a path with tilting axes, the group made its way to the platform. Police closed the doors and Chick raced along a private corridor leading out behind the stage, pushing Isis and Alyssum in front of him.

Chick had cut some peep-holes in the back of the stage which was tastefully draped with hangings of festered velvet. They sat there on some cushions and waited. Just a yard in front of them Heartre was getting ready to read his notes. An extraordinary radiance emanated from his ascetic athletic body and the throng, captivated by the overpowering charm of his slightest gesture, waited anx-iously for the starting signal.

Numerous were the cases of fainting due to intra-uterine exaltation which affected the female section of the audi-ence in particular and, from their hide-out, Alyssum, Isis and Chick could distinctly hear the accelerated breathing of the twenty-four gate-crashers who had stolen in under the stage and were quietly undressing to take up less space.

'Remember?' asked Alyssum, looking tenderly at Chick.

'Yes,' said Chick. 'That's where we first got to know each other . . .'

He leaned towards Alyssum and kissed her tenderly.

'Were you under there?' asked Isis.

'Mmm . . .' said Alyssum. 'It was lovely.'

'I bet it was,' said Isis. 'What's that, Chick?'

Chick was starting to open a big black box that he had with him.

'It's a recorder,' he said. 'I bought it specially for the lecture.'

'Oh!' said Isis. 'What a good idea! . . . Now we needn't bother to listen! . . .'

'Quite,' said Chick. 'And when we get home we can listen to it all night long if we like – although we won't because I don't want to spoil the records. I'll get copies made first and maybe I'll get "His Martyred Void" to make a commercial pressing for me.'

'It must have cost you a lot,' said Isis.

'Shhh! . . .' said Chick. 'That's not important.'

Alyssum sighed. Such a little little sigh that she was the only one to hear it . . . and even she did not hear it very clearly.

'We're off! . . .' said Chick. 'He's started. I put my mike amongst the others on the table so that nobody would notice.'

Jean Pulse opened his mouth. At first all that could be heard was the clicking of the cameras. Photographers and reporters from the cinema and the press were having the time of their lives. But one of them was knocked over backwards by the rebound from his camera and a horrible confusion ensued. His furious colleagues rushed to his aid and sprinkled him with magnesium powder. He disappeared in a blinding flash to the general satisfaction of all and the police carried off to prison the ones who were left.

'Marvellous!' said Chick. 'Now I'll be the only one with any record of what's happened!'

The audience which had been fairly well-behaved until then began to get worked up and showed its admiration for Heartre by repeated shouts and acclamations after every word he said – which made perfect understanding of what he was saying rather difficult.

'Don't try to grasp everything,' said Chick. 'We'll listen to the recording at our leisure.'

'Especially since we can't hear a thing here,' said Isis. 'His voice isn't as loud as a mouse's. By the way, have you heard from Chloe?'

'I've had a line from her,' said Alyssum.

'Did they get there safely?'

'Yes, but they're going to cut their honeymoon short. Chloe isn't very well,' said Alyssum.

'And how's Nicholas?' asked Isis.

'He's fine. Chloe said he's been misbehaving wickedly with the daughters of every hotel-keeper they've stayed with.'

'Nicholas is OK,' said Isis. 'I only wonder why he's a cook . . .'

'Yes,' said Chick, 'it is funny.'

'Why?' said Alyssum. And, twisting Chick's ear, she added, 'I think it's better than collecting Heartre's books.'

'Chloe isn't seriously ill, is she?' asked Isis.

'She didn't say what it was exactly,' said Alyssum. 'She just said her chest was hurting her.'

'Chloe's such a pretty girl,' said Isis. 'I can't imagine her being ill.'

'Oh!' whispered Chick, 'look! . . .'

Part of the ceiling was slowly lifting and a row of heads appeared. Daring admirers had just found their way in through the stained-glass window and had carried off this difficult and dangerous operation expertly. Others were pushing them from behind and the first lot were energetically gripping the edges of the raised cornice.

'They're quite right to raise the roof,' said Chick. 'This really is a terrific meeting! . . .'

Heartre had stood up and was showing the audience some samples of petrified vomit. The prettiest, containing sweetbreads, sauerkraut and cider, was an outstanding success.

People could hardly hear anything any more, even from behind the curtains where Isis, Alyssum and Chick were hiding.

'Well,' said Isis, 'when will they be back?'

'Tomorrow – or the day after,' said Alyssum.

'We haven't seen them for ages! . . .' said Isis.

'Not since they got married . . .' said Alyssum.

'It was such a lovely wedding,' concluded Isis.

'Yes,' said Chick. That was the night Nicholas took you home . . .'

Luckily the whole ceiling collapsed into the hall at that moment, so that Isis did not have to go into any further explanations. A thick dust rose. Amongst the rubbish, whitish creatures were staggering about, reeling and stumbling over each other, asphyxiated by the heavy cloud of powdered plaster which was floating over the debris. Heartre had stopped and was laughing heartily, slapping his sides, delighted to see so many people committed to this activity. He took a great swig of dust and started coughing like mad.

Chick frantically turned the knobs on his recorder. He produced a vivid green flash which took a dive into the floor like lightning and disappeared through a crack in the parquet. A second flash followed, then a third, and he switched off the current just as a horrible insect, covered all over in legs, crept out of the motor.

'No wonder!' he said. 'It's been choked by all the dust in the mike.'

The pandemonium in the hall had reached its peak. Heartre, parched dry, had even swallowed the carafe itself and, having just read his last page, was getting ready to go. Chick had a flash of inspiration.

'I'll show him out this way,' he said. 'You go first, and I'll follow.'

29

Nicholas stopped on his way through the corridor. The suns were definitely coming through very badly indeed. The yellow ceramic tiles seemed to be tarnished and hidden behind a veil of mist, and the rays, instead of bouncing back like bright buckshot, slurped on to the floor and oozed themselves out into thin dull puddles. The walls, dappled with sunshine, no longer shone evenly all over as they did before.

The mice did not seem to be particularly put out by the change – all except the grey one with the black whiskers whose deeply worried expression was immediately noticeable. Nicholas supposed that it must have been upset by the sudden and unexpected termination of the honeymoon and was missing the fun and games it was hoping to have had on the trip.

'You don't look very happy,' he said.

The mouse pulled a long face and nodded its whiskers towards the walls.

'Yes,' said Nicholas, 'it's not right. Things used to be better than this. I don't know what the matter can be . . .'

The mouse appeared to be thinking for a moment, then shook its head and threw up its arms in a gesture of hopeless helplessness.

'No, neither do I,' said Nicholas. 'I just don't understand. Even when you use polish, nothing happens. It must be something in the air . . .'

He stopped, thought, shook his head too, and then went on his way. The mouse folded its arms and absent-mindedly started chewing, then spat the gum out immediately because it was flavoured with cat-mint. The errand-boy had delivered the wrong sort.

In the dining-room Chloe was having lunch with Colin.

'Hallo!' said Nicholas. 'Feeling better?'

'Oho!' said Colin, 'so you've decided to talk like everyone else once again?'

'I haven't got my shoes on yet,' explained Nicholas.

'I don't feel so bad today,' said Chloe.

Her eyes were shining, her cheeks were rosy, and she seemed happy to be back home again.

'She's eaten half the chicken pie,' said Colin.

'Wonderful!' said Nicholas. '*And* I didn't get that recipe from ffroydde.'

'What would you like to do today, Chloe?' asked Colin.

'Yes,' said Nicholas, 'will you be eating early or late?'

'What I'd like to do is go out with both of you, and Isis and Chick and Alyssum, and go skating and round the shops and end up at a party somewhere,' said Chloe, 'and on the way I want to buy myself an ephemerald amethystle clockwork ring.'

'Good,' said Nicholas, 'then I'll get cracking in the kitchen straight away.'

'Do your work barefooted, Nicholas,' said Chloe. 'It's so much less tiring for us. And besides, you won't have to change out of your uniform to get ready then!'

'I'll go and get some pieces of eighty-eight from my doublezoon-box,' said Colin, 'while you telephone the clan, Chloe. We'll have a great day out.'

'I'll do the ringing straight away,' said Chloe.

She sprang up and went to the phone. She lifted the receiver and hooted like an owl to show that she wanted to be put through to Chick.

Nicholas cleared the table by pulling a little lever. The dirty crockery skidded down into the sink along a flat pneumatic tube hidden under the carpet. He went out of the room and back along the corridor.

The mouse, standing on its back legs, was scratching at one of the tarnished tiles with its tiny fingers. Where it had been scratching it was shining again like new.

'Well, well, well!' said Nicholas. 'So you've managed it! . . . that's marvellous!'

The mouse stopped, completely out of breath, and showed Nicholas its raw bleeding knuckles.

'Oh!' said Nicholas. 'You've hurt yourself! . . . Come on, don't do any more. After all, there's still plenty of sunshine left. Come along with me and I'll bandage you up . . .'

He put the exhausted mouse, with its half-closed eyelids, into his breast pocket, letting its poor little wounded paws hang out over the edge.

Humming a tune, Colin swiftly swivelled the knobs on

his chest of doublezoons. The worry of the last few days had disappeared and he felt as light-hearted as a mandarin orange. The chest was made of white marble inlaid with ivory, and the knobs were of seaweed-green sapphire. The pointer showed he had sixty thousand doublezoons left.

The lid swung open with a slick click, and the smile swept itself from Colin's face. The indicator, which for some reason had been jammed, after swivelling round two or three times, stayed fixed at thirty-five thousand doublezoons. Doing some quick mental arithmetic, he worked out a rough trial balance. Out of a hundred thousand, he had given twenty-five thousand to Chick to marry Alyssum, spent fifteen thousand on the car, five thousand on the wedding . . . and the rest had frittered itself away naturally. That cheered him a little. 'It's only normal,' he said out loud – and his voice sounded strangely unconvincing, even to himself . . .

He took as much as he needed, thought a moment, and then put half of it back with a sorrowful shrug, and locked the lid. The knobs rapidly swivelled round making a gay little noise like a chorus of castanets. He tapped the glass of the gold-barometer and checked that it showed correctly how much was inside.

Then he stood up. He stood still for a few moments, pondering. He was shocked by the large amounts he was having to spend to give Chloe the things he thought she deserved – but smiled when he thought of Chloe with her hair long and flowing first thing in the morning, and of the curves and contours of her body – in bed – under the sheet, and of the golden colour of her skin when he took the sheet away . . . and he sharply forced himself to think of his phynances again because it was far from being the right moment to be thinking of those other kinds of things . . .

Chloe was getting ready.

'Tell Nicholas to make some Satchmo sandwiches,' she said, 'so that we can go out straight away . . . I said we'd all meet at Isis's place.'

On the spur of the moment, Colin kissed her on the shoulder, and then ran to tell Nicholas. Nicholas had just finished bandaging the mouse and was making it a little pair of crutches out of twigs of bamboo.

'There we are,' he said, putting it down. 'Try walking on those till this evening, and then everything should be all right again.'

'What happened?' asked Colin, tickling the mouse behind the ear.

'It wanted to get the tiles in the corridor sparkling again,' said Nicholas. 'It managed it, but it hurt itself in the process.'

'You shouldn't worry about them,' said Colin. 'They'll get their shine back by themselves one day.'

'I don't know,' said Nicholas. 'It's very odd. It's as if they couldn't breathe properly.'

'They'll soon be back to normal,' said Colin . . . 'At least, I'm almost certain they will . . . Haven't they ever gone like it before?'

'No,' said Nicholas.

Colin stood for a few moments beside the kitchen window.

'Perhaps it's just wear and tear,' he said. 'We could try putting new ones down . . .'

'That would be very expensive,' said Nicholas.

'Yes,' said Colin. 'We might as well wait and see.'

'What did you want?' asked Nicholas.

'Don't do any cooking,' said Colin. 'Just make some Satchmo sandwiches . . . We're going out straight away.'

'OK then. I'll get dressed,' said Nicholas.

He put the mouse on the floor and it hobbled off towards the door, tottering between its little crutches, its black whiskers sticking out on either side.

30

The appearance of the street had completely altered since Colin and Chloe had been away. The leaves on the trees were enormous now, and the pale complexions of the houses had been lost under a gentle green shade prior to taking on the soft beige of summer. The pavement was growing soft and springy underfoot, and the air smelt of pomegranates and strawberries.

It was still fresh, but you could tell that fine weather was on the way by the blueness of the window-panes. Green and blue flowers – and some flowers that were between blue and blue – were growing all along the kerbs of the pavement, and the sap trickled round their slim stems with a light damp sound like a kiss between a pair of amorous snails.

Nicholas was the first one out. He was wearing a sports suit of warm mustard tweed over a roll-neck sweater with a Fair-Isle pattern based on the wood-engraving of a Salmon à la Glamis taken from page 607 of the Colour Supplement to ffroydde's *Household Management*. His crepe-soled cante-loupe leather shoes hardly bent the tops of the vegetation. He was careful to walk in the double tracks that had been cleared to let the traffic through.

Colin and Chloe followed him, Chloe holding Colin's

hand, breathing deeply the scented air. She was in a little white woollen dress, with a short jacket of leopard-skin which had been treated to elongate the spots and make them spread out in echoing overlapping ovals and curious optical patterns. Her spun hair flowed freely, exhaling a heady perfume of pink jasmine.

Colin, his eyes half-closed, let himself be guided by this perfume, and his lips trembled like the wings of a butterfly every time he breathed in. The fronts of the houses abandoned their severe rectitude to join with him and, as a result, the relaxed features of the street occasionally misled Nicholas, forcing him to stop and check up on their names at the corners.

'What shall we do first?' asked Colin.

'Go round the shops,' said Chloe. 'I've only got one dress left.'

'Don't you want to get one from Miss Hart and Miss Nell as usual?' said Colin.

'No,' said Chloe. 'I want to go round the shops and buy some ready-made dresses – and things and things and things!'

'Isis will be thrilled to see you again, Nicholas,' said Colin.

'Oh, will she? Why?' asked Nicholas.

'I've no idea . . .'

They swerved into Sidney Bechet Street – and they were there. The housekeeper was sitting at the door in a mechanical rocking-chair whose engine popped to the rhythm of a polka. It was all rather old-fashioned and charming.

Isis greeted them. Chick and Alyssum were there already. Isis was wearing a red dress and smiled at Nicholas. She kissed Chloe and they all permutated their interkissings for a few moments.

'You look so well, Chloe darling,' said Isis. 'I thought you were ill. But I can see you aren't.'

'I'm much better,' said Chloe. 'Nicholas and Colin looked after me marvellously.'

'How are your little cousins?' asked Nicholas.

Isis blushed to her eyebrows.

'They take turns to ask me about you every other day,' she said.

'They're lovely girls,' said Nicholas, half-turning away, 'but you are firmer.'

'Yes . . .' said Isis.

'And the honeymoon?' said Chick.

'Went off very well,' said Colin. 'The road was terrible to start with, but we managed to get over it.'

'It was all lovely,' said Chloe, 'except for the snow . . .'

She put her hand on her heart.

'What are we going to do?' asked Alyssum.

'I could tell you about Heartre's lecture, if you like,' said Chick.

'Have you bought many books of his while we've been away?' asked Colin.

'Oh, no! Not many . . .' said Chick.

'And how's work?' asked Colin.

'Oh! . . . All right . . .' said Chick. 'I've got a pal who takes over when I have to go out.'

'For nothing?' asked Colin.

'Well . . . Almost,' said Chick. 'Do you want to go to the kspot straight away?'

'o, we're going to the shops first,' said Chloe 'But if the ant to go skating . . .'

'That's a good idea,' said Colin.

'I'll go round the shops with the girls,' said Nicholas. 'I've got some shopping to do too.'

'That's fine then,' said Isis. 'But let's hurry so we'll have time for a moment or two on the rink afterwards.'

31

Colin and Chick had been skating for an hour and the ice was beginning to get crowded. The same girls and the same boys were constantly going round and round, forever falling over in the same way and being swept away by the sweeper-serfs and their squeegees. The risk-jockey had just lifted from the turntable a chorus that the regulars had been learning by heart for weeks. He replaced it by the flip-side – an action that was thoroughly expected as his habits were beginning to become well-known. But the record suddenly stopped and a stentorian voice could be heard over all the loud-speakers but one, which stubbornly went on with the music. The voice asked Mr Colin if he would *go* to the Manager's Office as he was wanted on the telephone.

'Whatever can that be for?' said Colin.

He flew to the edge of the rink, followed by Chick, and landed on the rubber matting. He grabbed the rail and rushed into the control cabin where the microphone was.

The risk-jockey was scrubbing the surface of a well-worn record from the top of the charts with a wire-brush to get rid of the scratches.

'Hello!' said Colin, picking up the phone.

He listened.

Chick watched him. Firstly he looked shocked, and then turned the same colour as the ice.

'Is it something serious?' he asked.

Colin made a sign asking him to keep quiet.

'I'll be straight there,' he said, and hung up.

The sides of the cabin closed in and he just managed to squeeze out, followed closely by Chick, before he was crushed. He twisted his ankles with every step. He called to one of the attendants.

'Open my cubicle for me quickly. No. 309.'

'Mine too. No. 311,' said Chick.

The attendant dawdled along. Colin looked round, saw him ten yards behind and waited till he had caught him up. Taking brutal aim with his skate, he gave him a savage karate chop under the chin and the attendant's head flew off and landed on the top of one of the ventilation shafts while Colin took the key which the body was still absent-mindedly clutching in its hand. Colin opened a cubicle, kicked the trunk inside, spat on it and dashed off to No. 309. Chick slammed the door.

'Whatever's the matter?' he asked breathlessly when he got there.

Colin had already taken off his skates and put on his shoes.

'It's Chloe,' said Colin. 'She's been taken ill.'

'Seriously?'

'I don't know,' said Colin. 'She's fainted.'

He was ready and rushed out.

'Where are you going?' cried Chick.

'Home! . . .' shouted Colin, and he disappeared, followed by the reinforced echoes of the concrete stairs.

At the other end of the rinkunabula the half-suffocated

maintenance men from the ventilation plant were crawling out because the air-conditioning had collapsed. They fell down, exhausted, all round the rink.

Chick, stupefied, one skate in his hand, looked in bewilderment at the spot where Colin had disappeared.

Under the door of Cubicle No. 128, a thin bubbly trickle of blood was stickily oozing out, and the red liquid began to drip on to the ice in fat heavy steaming drops.

32

He ran like mad, seeing the people slowly toppling over to right and left like ninepins, making soft plopping noises on the pavements like a bombardment of empty cardboard boxes.

Colin ran on and on and on. The steep horizon, squeezed into a narrow space between the houses, was whizzing towards him. It was growing dark underfoot. A night of amorphous and inorganic black cotton-wool. And a sky without colour; a ceiling. Another sharp angle – arid he ran to the peak of the pyramid, his heart held by less gloomy visions of the night. But there were still two or three more streets to cross before he would be home.

Chloe was lying weightlessly on the fine bed where they had spent their wedding night. Her eyes were open, but she was breathing badly. Alyssum was with her. Isis was helping Nicholas who had searched through ffroydde for a pick-me-up, and the mouse was chopping up exotic herbs and seeds with its sharp teeth for a special night-cap.

But Colin knew nothing about this. He was running and

he was scared. Why can't we always be together? Things were always happening to alarm us. Perhaps it was an accident. She's been run over. She'll be in bed. I won't be allowed to see her. They'll stop me going in. But you don't really think I'd be afraid of seeing my darling Chloe? I must see her, whatever they may say. No, Colin, don't go in. Perhaps she's only got a minor injury – and tomorrow it will all be over. We'll go out to the park again together, and sit on the bench again, holding hands, her hair mingling with mine. I still steal her pillow and have pillow-fights with her every night. Hers is too hard for her. It stays stiff under her head, so I take it because it smells of her hair. Never again to smell the sweet smell of her hair . . .

The pavement rose straight up to meet him. He stepped over it with a giant stride and he was on the first floor. He went in, opened the door – and all was calm and quiet. There was nobody in black, no priests. The carpets and their blue-grey patterns were all at peace. Nicholas said, 'It's nothing to worry about,' and Chloe smiled. She was happy that he was back home again.

33

Chloe's hand, warm and relaxed, rested confidently in Colin's. She was looking at him, reassuring him with her clear bewildered eyes. Underneath the platform in the bedroom worries were mounting up on top of each other, eager to stifle the ones lower in the pile. Chloe was conscious of an opaque force inside her body. She did not know how to struggle with the opposing presence in her chest and fight back. When she dared she coughed, to try to dislodge the enemy that was clutching on to something deep inside her. When she breathed deeply she felt she was being sacrificed alive to the featureless wrath of the enemy and its insidious evil. But she hardly seemed to be breathing and the smooth sheets over her long naked legs seemed to pour calm oil on each of her troubled movements. At her side, Colin watchfully and tenderly looked down at her. It was growing dark in the shape of concentric ripples round the minute luminous centre of the lighted lamp that was set in the wall at the side of the bed, and screened by a round plaque of unpolished crystal.

'Put on some music for me, Colin,' said Chloe. 'Put on something that you like.'

'It will tire you to listen,' said Colin.

His voice came from far away. He looked ill. His heart filled every corner of his chest, and he had only just realized it.

'Of course it won't,' said Chloe. 'Please! . . .'

Colin got up, scrambled down the little oak ladder and went over to the panel that controlled loud-speakers in all the rooms. He switched on the one in the bedroom.

'What have you put on?' asked Chloe.

She smiled. She knew perfectly well.

'Remember?' said Colin.

'I remember . . .'

'You're sure you're not in pain?'

'It doesn't hurt very much . . .'

At the spot where a river joins the ocean there is a barrier that is very difficult to navigate. Wrecked ships dance helplessly in the great eddies of foam. Between the night outside and the light of the lamp, memories flowed back from the darkness of the past, banging against the light and, immersed in its glow, gleaming and transparent, flaunted their white fronts and their silver backs.

Chloe tried to sit up a little.

'Come back and sit by my side . . .'

Colin went up close to her and snuggled himself across the bed so that Chloe's head rested in the hollow of his left arm. The lace of her light nightdress made a frivolous interlaced pattern over her golden skin, tenderly broken by the rising of her breasts. Chloe's hand clung to Colin's shoulder.

'You're not angry with me? . . .'

'Angry? Why?'

'Because you've got such a stupid wife . . .'

He kissed the hollow of her worried shoulder.

'Put your arm back inside, Chloe. You'll catch cold.'

'I don't feel cold,' said Chloe. 'Listen to the record.'

There was something unearthly in the way Johnny Hodges played. Something inexplicable, yet perfectly sensual. Sensuality in its purest state, quite separate from anything physical.

The corners of the room softened and curved with the music. Colin and Chloe were now lying in the centre of a sphere.

'What was that?' asked Chloe.

'It was "The Mood to be Wooed",' said Colin.

'That's just how I felt,' said Chloe. 'But how will the doctor be able to get in here with a shape like this?'

34

Nicholas went to open the door. The doctor was standing on the step.

'I'm the doctor,' he said.

'Smashing,' said Nicholas. 'If you would be good enough to follow me . . .'

He lured him along behind him.

'There,' he said when they were in the kitchen, 'taste that and tell me what you think.'

A peculiarly coloured brew, verging towards Caucasian purple and bladder green with a slight bias towards chrome blue was fizzing in a vitrified receptacle of silicon, soda and lime-juice.

'What is it?' asked the doctor.

'A beverage . . .' said Nicholas.

'I know that . . .' said the doctor, 'but what does it do?'

'It picks you up,' said Nicholas.

The doctor picked up the glass, passed it under his nose, smelled it, gave a broad grin, inhaled deeply, tasted it, then swallowed it down and held his stomach in both hands, letting his little black bag drop.

'Does it work?' said Nicholas.

'Wow! . . . It certainly does,' said the doctor. 'It could massacre an army . . . Are you a vet?'

'No,' said Nicholas, 'just a cook . . . Well then, so it works, does it?'

'It's not bad,' said the doctor. 'I feel like a boy again . . .'

'Come and see the patient,' said Nicholas, 'now that you've been disinfected.'

The doctor set off, but in the wrong direction.

He was far from being master of his movements.

'Ho, hum!' said Nicholas. 'Well now! . . . I hope you'll be fit enough to examine the patient . . .'

'Of course,' said the doctor. 'But I'd like to have a second opinion, so I've asked Gnawknuckle to come along too . . .'

'Good,' said Nicholas. 'In that case, come this way.'

He opened the door leading to the fire escape.

'Go down three floors and turn right. Just go straight in and you'll be there . . .'

'OK,' said the doctor . . .

He started on his way down and suddenly stopped.

'But where will I be?'

'Why, there! . . .' said Nicholas.

'Oh! Good! . . .' said the doctor.

Nicholas closed the door. Colin came in.

'What was all that?' he asked.

'A doctor. He seemed stupid, so I've got rid of him.'

'But we need one,' said Colin.

'Of course,' said Nicholas. 'Gnawknuckle's on his way.'

'That's better,' said Colin.

A bell tinkled again.

'Don't bother,' said Colin. 'I'll go.'

In the corridor the mouse ran up his leg and perched on his right shoulder. He hurried and opened the door for the professor.

'Good evening!' said the latter.

He was all dressed in black, except for a blinding yellow shirt.

'Physiologically,' he declared, 'black over a yellow background provides the maximum contrast. I might add that it doesn't tire the eyes, either; and it also prevents the wearer being run over in heavy traffic.'

'Indeed,' said Colin, nodding his approval.

Professor Gnawknuckle must have been about fifty. The inches round his waist were exactly the same as his age. He was very fussy about ensuring that neither should exceed the other. He had a clean-shaven face with a little pointed beard and non-committal specs.

'Would you like to come with me?' said Colin.

'I'm not sure,' said the professor. 'I'm thinking about it . . .'

He thought about it and went.

'Who is it that's ill?'

'Chloe,' said Colin.

'Ah!' said the professor, 'that reminds me of a tune . . .'

'Yes,' said Colin. 'It's the same one.'

'First,' concluded Gnawknuckle, 'let's go and see her. You should have told me sooner. What's wrong with her?'

'I don't know,' said Colin.

'Neither do I,' confessed the professor. 'We might as well face facts.'

'But you will find out?' asked Colin anxiously.

'I may do,' said Professor Gnawknuckle, doubtfully. 'I haven't examined her yet . . .'

'Come on then . . .' said Colin.

'Yes, yes, yes . . .' said the professor.

Colin led him to the bedroom door and suddenly remembered something.

'Mind how you go in,' he said. 'It's round.'

'Yes, yes, I'm used to that,' said Gnawknuckle. 'She's pregnant? . . .'

'Oh, no!' said Colin, 'don't be silly . . . The room's round!'

'Completely round?' asked the professor. 'Have you been playing an Ellington record then?'

'Yes, we have,' said Colin.

109

'I've got some at home too,' said Gnawknuckle. 'D'you know "Slap Happy"?'

'I prefer . . .' began Colin. Then he remembered that Chloe was waiting, and pushed the professor into the room.

'Good evening,' said the professor. He went up the ladder.

'Good evening,' replied Chloe. 'How do you do?'

'Floundering flukes,' answered the professor, 'my liver puts me through it at times, you know. Do you know what it's like?'

'No,' said Chloe.

'Of course not,' replied the professor. 'You haven't got anything wrong with your liver, have you?'

He went up to Chloe and felt her hand.

'A trifle warm, eh? . . .'

'I can't tell.'

'Hmm,' said the professor. 'But that's a red herring.'

He sat on the edge of the bed.

'I'll sound you, if you don't mind.'

'Go ahead,' said Chloe.

The professor took an amplified stethoscope out of his little black bag and put it on Chloe's back.

'Start counting,' he said.

Chloe counted.

'That's not right,' said the doctor. 'It's twenty-seven that comes after twenty-six!'

'Of course it does,' said Chloe. 'I'm sorry.'

'That's enough, anyway,' said the doctor. 'Have you been coughing?'

'Yes,' said Chloe, and she coughed.

'What's wrong with her, doctor?' asked Colin. 'Is it serious?'

'Well! . . .' said the professor, 'she's got something the matter with her right lung. But I don't know what it is . . .'

'What can we do?' asked Colin.

'She'll have to come and see me for a more detailed examination,' said the professor.

'I don't very much like the idea of taking her out, doctor,' said Colin. 'Suppose she has another attack like the one she had this afternoon?'

'Don't worry,' said the professor. 'It isn't serious. I'll give you a prescription, but you must be sure to take it.'

'Of course, doctor,' said Chloe.

She put her hand to her mouth and began coughing.

'Don't cough,' said Gnawknuckle.

'Try not to cough, darling,' said Colin.

'I can't help it,' said Chloe, between coughs.

'There's a funny kind of music you can hear in her lung,' said the professor.

He seemed rather puzzled and put out.

'Is it normal, doctor?' asked Colin.

'To a certain degree . . .' replied the professor.

He pulled his little beard and it sprang back on to his chin with a sharp snap.

'When shall we come and see you, doctor?' asked Colin.

'In three days time,' said the professor. 'I'll have got my apparatus working again by then.'

'Don't you often use it?' asked Chloe this time.

'No,' said the professor. 'I much prefer making scale models of aeroplanes. But people are always pestering me so I've been on the same one for a year now and I can't seem to find the time to finish it. It gets exasperating after a while! . . .'

'It must do,' said Colin.

'They're sharks,' said the professor. 'It amuses me to

compare myself to the poor shipwrecked mariner whose slumbers are watched by voracious monsters waiting for the precise moment to capsize his fragile craft.'

'How poetic,' said Chloe, and she laughed, very quietly so that she would not start coughing again.

'Be careful, honey child,' said the professor, putting his hand on her shoulder. 'It's a stupidly poetic image because in the *New Scientist* for 16 May 1931 it's clearly stated that, contrary to current opinion, only three or four of the thirty-five known species of sharks are man-eaters. And even they only attack if they are attacked first . . .'

'What a lot of things you know, doctor,' said Chloe, full of admiration.

She rather liked this doctor.

'What a lot of things the *New Scientist* knows,' said the doctor, '– not me! And, on that word, I shall bid you Good-Night.'

He gave Chloe a big kiss on her right cheek, patted her on the shoulder and went down the little ladder. His right foot got tangled round his left foot, his left foot round the bottom rung, and he tumbled all the way down.

'You have to know the knack of this gadget,' he remarked to Colin, rubbing his back vigorously.

'I'm sorry,' said Colin.

'And anyway,' added the professor, 'there's something lugubrious about this spherical room. Try putting on "Slap Happy" – that ought to bring it back to shape. Otherwise I should try planing it.'

'Orders understood,' said Colin. 'Can I offer you one for the road?'

'OK,' said the professor. 'Bye-bye, my dear,' he called to Chloe, before going out of the room.

Chloe was still smiling. From down below you could see her sitting on the big low bed as if she were on a trampoline, theatrically lit by the bedside lamp. The rays of light filtered through her hair with the luminosity and colour of sunshine through fresh young blades of grass, and the light that had been close to her skin touched with gold those objects that it went on to illuminate.

'You've got a very pretty wife,' the professor said to Colin when they were out of the room.

'Yes, I have,' said Colin.

Tears suddenly began to run down his cheeks because he knew that Chloe was in pain.

'Now, now,' said the professor, 'you're putting me in an embarrassing position . . . I'll have to do something to make you feel better too . . .'

He delved into the inside pocket of his jacket and pulled out a little notebook bound in real leather.

'Look, this is mine.'

'Your what?' asked Colin, doing his best to remain patient.

'My wife,' explained the professor.

Colin opened the notebook out of politeness, and then burst out laughing.

'There! You see!' said the professor. 'It never fails. They all laugh. But you must tell me . . . What is there so funny about her?'

'I . . . I don't . . . know,' burbled Colin, and doubled over, a helpless prey to a seizure of extreme high hilarity.

The professor took back his wallet.

'You're all the same,' he said. 'You think a woman has to be pretty . . . And what about that drink? Am I still going to get it?'

35

Colin, closely followed by Chick, pushed open the door of the remedy shop. It went 'Ding!' and the glass in the door shattered into a terrifyingly complex jigsaw over a display of phials and laboratory instruments.

Disturbed by the noise, the crapothecary looked up. He was thin, tall and old, and his head sported an erect white mane like a crown.

He sprang to his counter, grabbed the telephone and dialled a number with that swiftness that can only be acquired as the result of many years of experience.

'Hello!' he said.

His voice was like a fog-horn, and the floor around his long flat black feet flowed evenly backwards and forwards while showers of spray hit the counter and bounced off again.

'Hello! Gershwin House? Would you come and put some new glass in my shop door? In fifteen minutes? . . . Hurry then, in case another customer comes in . . . OK . . .'

He put down the phone and it struggled to clamber home over the dial.

'What can I do for you, gentlemen?'

'Make up this prescription . . .' suggested Colin.

The chemist snatched the sheet of paper, drew a pair of eyes, a nose and a mouth on it, and then applied eye-shadow powder and lipstick to them.

'That's done!' he said, blacking one of the eyes with a rubber stamp proclaiming his name and address.

'Come back this evening at six of the clock and your remedy will be ready.'

'We're in,' said Colin, 'a great hurry.'

'We'd like,' said Chick, 'to have it straight away.'

'If you'd,' replied the salesman, 'like to wait, then I'll see what I can do.'

Colin and Chick sat and waited on a long seat uphol-stered in purple plush that was facing the counter. The shopkeeper bobbed down behind his counter and disap-peared through a secret door, crawling away almost silently. The shuffling of his long thin body over the parquet grew fainter and fainter and finally faded away into nothing.

They looked at the walls. On long shelves of crinkled green copper were rows of bottles full of liniments for lin-eaments, salted balm-cakes, peppermints and mustard plas-ters. From the end jar on each shelf emanated a fluorescent barrier. In a conical recipient of thick smoked glass swollen tadpoles were helterskeltering down in spirals. When they reached the bottom they darted off again up to the surface and began their eccentric gyration all over again, leaving a whitish wake of ruffled water behind them. At the side of an aquarium several yards long the shopkeeper had set up a laboratory bench to carry on experiments on nozzle-frogs. Here and there several rejected frogs were lying around, each of their four hearts still feebly beating.

On the wall behind Chick and Colin there was a vast fresco showing the remedy-man in process of fornication with his mother, wearing Lucrezia Borgia's racing outfit. On tables there were multitudes of pill-making machines and some of them were working – although not very quickly.

The pills, coming out through an exhaust-pipe of blue glass, were caught by wax hands which put them into little paper bags and wrapped them up.

Colin stood up to look more carefully at the machine

nearest to him and lifted up its rusty tin cover. Inside it, a composite animal, half-flesh, half-metal, was rapidly killing itself by swallowing the basic materials and expulsing them in the form of little round pills.

'Come and look, Chick,' said Colin.

'What?' asked Chick.

'There's something very peculiar here! . . .' said Colin.

Chick looked. The animal had an elongated jaw with a rapid lateral movement. Under its transparent skin, thin tubular steel ribs could be seen and a digestive tract which seemed to be working in slow motion.

'It's a modified rabbit,' said Chick.

'D'you think so?'

'Yes. Everybody's doing it,' said Chick. 'It's the latest thing. You just keep the bits you need. There, you see, he's kept the mechanism of the digestive system, but flung out the chemical part and the metabolism. It's much more simple than making pills with a mould in the old way.'

'What does it feed on?' asked Colin.

'Chromium carrots,' said Chick. 'They used to make them in the factory where I worked when I first left school. Then it's given the ingredients of the pills . . .'

'It's a fine invention,' said Colin, 'and it makes very pretty pills.'

'Yes,' said Chick. 'They're as round as can be.'

'Tell me,' said Colin, going back to sit down.

'What?' asked Chick.

'How much of the twenty-five thousand doublezoons I gave you before I went on my honeymoon have you got left?'

'Er! . . .' replied Chick.

'It's about time you made up your mind to marry

Alyssum. It's wearing her out carrying on the way you carry on!!!'

'I know . . .' replied Chick.

'Well, you must still have about twenty thousand double-zoons. That ought to be plenty to get married on, all the same . . .'

'Yes, but . . .' said Chick.

He stopped because it was hard to come out with it.

'Yes, but what?' insisted Colin. 'You're not the only one with money problems.'

'I know,' said Chick.

'Well then?' said Colin.

'Well,' said Chick, 'I'm afraid I've only got three thousand two hundred doublezoons left . . .'

Colin suddenly felt very low. Shadowy objects with dull blunt spikes were going round and round inside his head, making a noise like the distant tide coming in from afar. He sat up on the seat.

'It can't be true,' he said.

He was weary, as weary as if he had been hounded and whipped over a long steeplechase.

'It can't be true . . .' he repeated . . . 'You're leading me on.'

'I'm sorry . . .' said Chick.

Chick was standing up. With the tip of his finger he was scratching the corner of the nearest table. Pills were rolling out of the glass exhaust making a noise like the clicking of billiard-balls, and the scrumpling of the paper-bags by the dummy hands created a portrait in muzak of a West End-ian piscatorial parlour.

'But what did you do with it all?' asked Colin. 'Bought loads of Heartre,' said Chick. He felt in his pocket.

'Look at this. I found it only yesterday. Isn't it marvellous?'

It was *A Bouquet of Belches* bound in coarse-grained morocco, with coloured plates by Kierkegaard.

Colin took the book and looked at it, but he did not see the pages. He could see the eyes of Alyssum, on the day he was married, and the look of sad wonder that filled them as she admired Chloe's dress. But Chick wouldn't understand that. His eyes never rose so high.

'What on earth can I say to you? . . .' murmured Colin. 'So you've spent the lot? . . .'

'I got two of his manuscripts last week,' said Chick, his voice trembling with suppressed excitement. 'And I've already recorded seven of his lectures . . .'

'Yes, yes . . .' said Colin.

'Why did you ask me?' said Chick. 'Alyssum doesn't care whether I marry her or not. She's happy as she is. You know I like her a lot, especially as she's crazy about Heartre too!'

One of the machines seemed to have got out of control. A cataract of pills tumbled out and there was a blinding violet flash when they fell into the paper bag.

'What's happening?' said Colin. 'Is it going to explode?'

'I don't think so,' said Chick. 'All the same, don't go too close.'

Somewhere in the distance they could hear a door closing, and the remedy-man suddenly popped up behind the counter.

'I kept you waiting,' he said.

'Don't worry about that,' Colin reassured him.

'But I must . . .' said the shopkeeper. 'I did it on purpose. I have to do it to keep up my position.'

'One of your machines seems to have got out of control . . .' said Colin, pointing to the one that was going crazy.

'Aha! . . .' said the remedy-man.

He leant over, took a rifle from under the counter, put it to his shoulder, carefully took aim and fired. The machine sprang into the air, did a somersault and fell back exhausted.

'It wasn't anything,' said the salesman. 'Now and again the rabbit gets the upper hand over the steel and has to be put down.'

He picked up the machine, pressed on the base plate to extract the juices, and hung it on a nail.

'Here's your remedy,' he said, taking a box from his pocket. 'Be careful, it's very potent. Don't take more than it says on the label.'

'Fine!' said Colin. 'Tell me, what do you think it's for?'

'Couldn't say . . .' replied the shopkeeper.

He plunged a long hand with twisted nails into his white mop.

'It might be for all kinds of things . . .' he concluded. 'But most ordinary plants wouldn't stand up to it for very long.'

'Oh, I see!' said Colin. 'How much do I owe you?'

'It's very expensive,' said the shopkeeper. 'You ought to cosh me and run off without paying . . .'

'Oh!' said Colin, 'I'm too tired.'

'Well, it's two doublezoons,' said the shopkeeper.

Colin took out his crocket.

'You know,' said the shopkeeper, 'it's really daylight robbery.'

'I don't mind . . .' said Colin in a lifeless voice.

He paid up and went. Chick followed him.

'Don't be a fool,' said the remedy-man, going to the door with them. 'I'm very old and I wouldn't put up a fight.'

'I'm sorry, I can't spare the time,' mumbled Colin.

'That's not true,' said the shopkeeper. 'Or you wouldn't have waited so long . . .'

'I've got the remedy now,' said Colin. 'Good-bye.' He walked across the street diagonally in order to save his strength.

'You know,' said Chick, 'just because I'm not marrying Alyssum, it doesn't mean that I'm going to leave her . . .'

'Oh!' said Colin. 'I can't give you any advice . . . After all, it's your business . . .'

'That's life,' said Chick.

'It isn't,' said Colin.

36

The wind blew a path between the leaves, took it, and came out on the other side of the trees loaded with the perfume of buds and flowers. People *were* walking on air and breathing more deeply because there was plenty of freshness about. The sun slowly unfolded its rays and chanced them in the sky, cautiously prying into places which it could not strike directly, bending them round curved and ornate angles, but banging against very black things and drawing them back immediately as if it were a clockwork ormolu octopus made by Fabergé. Its immense burning carcass came slowly closer and closer until, finally immobile, it began to turn the waters of the continent to vapour and all the clocks struck three.

Colin was reading a story to Chloe. It was a love story in which everybody lived happily ever after. They were up to the part where the hero and heroine were sending letters to each other.

'Why is it so slow? . . .' said Chloe. 'Things normally happen quicker than that . . .'

'Are you used to things like that?' asked Colin.

He sharply nipped the end of a ray of sunshine that was about to jab Chloe straight in the eye. It curled away coyly and started limping over the furniture in the bedroom.

Chloe blushed.

'No, I'm not used to things like that . . .' she said shyly, 'but it seems to me . . .'

Colin closed the book.

'You're right, my little Chloe.'

He got up and sat on the bed.

'It's time for one of your pills.'

Chloe shuddered.

'They're so nasty,' she said. 'Have I got to take them?'

'I think you should,' said Colin. 'We're going to the doctor's tonight – and at last we'll know what the trouble is. But you must take one of your pills now. Perhaps he'll give you something different then . . .'

'These are horrible,' said Chloe.

'Try to be sensible.'

'It's just as if two savage animals were fighting inside my chest when I take one. And anyway, it isn't true . . . it's no good trying to be sensible . . .'

'It's more fun not to be, but sometimes you just have to,' said Colin.

He opened the little box.

'They're a horrid colour,' said Chloe, 'and they smell bad.'

'They are strange, I know,' said Colin, 'but you must take them.'

'Look,' said Chloe. 'They're moving! You can seem to see through them and I'm sure there's something alive in the middle.'

'If there is, it won't live long in the water you have to drink with them,' said Colin.

'That's silly – it might be a fish! . . .'

Colin began to laugh.

'Well, if it is, then it should help build up your strength.'

He leaned across and kissed her.

'Hurry up and take it, Chloe baby. Be nice!'

'I'll do my best,' said Chloe, 'but promise to kiss me again afterwards!'

'Of course I will,' said Colin, 'if you're not ashamed of kissing such a wicked husband . . .'

'You do look rather diabolical,' said Chloe, teasing.

'I can't help it.'

Colin pulled a long face.

'I don't get enough sleep,' he went on.

'Kiss me, little Colin. I'm very wicked too. Give me two pills to make me good.'

'You're crazy,' said Colin. 'One's enough. Just swallow. Swallow . . .'

Chloe closed her eyes. She went pale and lifted her hand to her chest.

'It's gone,' she said, with great difficulty. 'And now it's going to start all over again . . .'

Little beads of perspiration appeared at the edges of her brilliant hair.

Colin sat by her side and put his arm round her neck. She grabbed his hand between both of hers, whimpering.

'Take it easy, Chloe baby,' said Colin. 'You must try . . .'

'It hurts . . .' murmured Chloe.

Tears as big as her eyes appeared at the corners of her lids and traced cold tracks across her soft round cheeks.

37

'I can't stand any more . . .' murmured Chloe.

She had both feet on the ground and was trying to stand up.

'It's no good,' she said . . . 'I'm so weak.'

Colin went over and lifted her up. She held on to his shoulders.

'Hold me, Colin. I'm going to fall!'

'It's being in bed that's made you so weak . . .' said Colin.

'No,' said Chloe. 'It's that old quack's pills.'

She tried to stand alone, but tottered. Colin caught her and she dragged him down on to the bed with her.

'I feel fine like this,' said Chloe. 'Stay here with me. It's such a long time since we've been to bed together.'

'You mustn't,' said Colin.

'But I must. Kiss me. I'm your wife, aren't I?'

'Of course you are,' said Colin. 'But you're not well.'

'It isn't my fault,' said Chloe, and her mouth trembled ever so slightly, as if she were going to cry.

Colin held her close and kissed her very tenderly, as he would have kissed a flower.

'Do that again,' said Chloe. 'And not just on my cheek. Don't you love me any more? Don't you want a little wife any more?'

He held her still more tightly in his arms. She was warm and moist and full of perfume. Like a bottle from a boutique in a box padded with white satin.

'Yes please,' said Chloe, stretching herself out . . . 'Yes, please, do that again . . .'

38

'We'll be late,' said Colin.

'Don't worry,' said Chloe, 'we'll blame it on your watch.'

'You really don't want to go by car? . . .'

'No . . .' said Chloe. 'I want to be seen walking in the street with you.'

'But it's a long way to go!'

'I don't mind,' said Chloe . . . 'When you . . . kissed me just now, it made me fit again. I feel like walking a little.'

'I'll tell Nicholas to come and pick us up in the car afterwards, shall I?' suggested Colin.

'Oh! Yes, please . . .'

To go to the doctor's she had put on a friendly little blue dress, very low cut with a V-neck, and a little ocelot jacket with a hat to match. Dyed serpent-skin accessories completed the outfit.

'Come along, pussy!' said Colin.

'It isn't cat,' sulked Chloe. 'It's ocelot.'

'That's far too hard for me to spell,' said Colin.

They went out of the bedroom and into the hall. Chloe stopped by the window.

'What's happened here? It's not as bright as it used to be . . .'

'Of course it is,' said Colin. 'It's full of sunshine!'

'It isn't,' said Chloe. 'I can remember clearly that the sun used to come up to that pattern on the carpet, and now it only goes as far as this . . . !'

'It depends on the time of day,' said Colin.

'No, it doesn't depend on the time of day, because it was exactly at the same time as it is now! . . .'

'Then we'll take another look tomorrow at the same time,' said Colin.

'No, look now. It used to come up to the seventh repeat of the pattern. And now it's only on the fifth . . .'

'Come along,' said Colin. 'We're late.'

Chloe smiled at herself as she went past the big mirror in the tiled corridor. Her trouble couldn't be serious, and from now on they would go out for lots of walks together. He would get his doublezoons straightened out and find that he had enough left for them to lead a very pleasant life. Perhaps he might even go out to work . . .

The lock gave a steely click and the door closed behind them. Chloe held on to his arm. She was taking light little steps. Colin took one for every two of hers.

'I'm happy,' said Chloe. 'The sun is shining and the trees smell good!'

'Of course!' said Colin. 'Spring is here!'

'Is it?' said Chloe, giving him a wicked wink.

They turned to the right. There were two buildings to go past before reaching the medical district. A hundred yards farther on they could begin to smell the anaesthetics. On windy days the smell came even closer. The pavements were different here. They were wide flat canals, covered over with concrete grilles and narrowly spaced bars. Under the bars ran streams of antiseptic and ether, dragging drifting swabs of cotton-wool stained with damp and pus – and occasionally with blood – along with them. Long filaments of semi-coagulated blood tinged the volatile flux here and there, and shreds of half-rotten flesh twisted over themselves and slowly rolled away like melting icebergs that had grown too soft. The atmosphere was full of the smell of ether. Strips of gauze and dressings were swept along by the current too, loosely unwinding their sleepy spirals. At the side of every house a chute came straight down into the canal. Each doctor's speciality could be told by carefully watching the orifice at the bottoms of these tubes for a few moments. A rolling eye tumbled down one of them, looked at them for a minute or two, and then disappeared under a large sheet of spongy red cotton-wool like a dying jellyfish.

'I don't like this,' said Chloe. 'The air may be very healthy, but it isn't very easy on the eye . . .'

'No,' said Colin.

'Let's walk in the middle of the road.'

'Fine,' said Colin. 'But we'll get run over.'

'I was wrong to say no to the car,' said Chloe. 'I've got no legs left.'

'You're lucky he doesn't live in the middle of the big surgical centre . . .'

'Be quiet!' said Chloe. 'Are we nearly there?'

She suddenly started coughing again and Colin turned pale.

'Please don't cough, Chloe! . . .' he begged. 'I'm trying, Colin . . .' she said, restraining herself with tremendous difficulty.

'Don't cough . . . We're there . . . Here it is.'

Professor Gnawknuckle's sign was an immense jaw swallowing a fist so voraciously that only the elbow was left sticking out. It amused Chloe. She laughed very quietly, very low, because she was scared to cough any more. All round the walls were illuminated coloured photos of the miraculous cures performed by the professor, although the lights weren't working at that moment.

'Look,' said Colin. 'He's a big specialist. The other houses haven't got such fancy decorations.'

'It only proves that he's got lots of money,' said Chloe.

'Or lots of taste . . .' said Colin. 'It's very artistic.'

'Yes,' said Chloe. 'Just like a high-class butcher's.'

They went in and found they were in a large round vestibule all gleaming white. A nurse came up.

'Do you have an appointment?' she asked.

'Yes,' said Colin. 'We may be a little late . . .'

'It doesn't matter,' said the nurse haughtily. 'The professor has finished operating for today. Would you follow me, please?'

They did, and the sharp high sound of their footsteps echoed on the polished floor. There was a set of doors in the circular wall, and the nurse led them to the one which had a miniature copy of the giant swinging sign outside stuck on it in embossed gold. She opened the door and stood back to let them in. They pushed a massive transparent inner door and found themselves in the professor's surgery. He was standing in front of the window, shampooing his beard with a toothbrush dipped in extract of opoponax.

He turned round when he heard them and went up to Chloe, holding out his hand.

'Well, now, how do you feel today?'

'Those pills were terrible,' said Chloe.

The professor's face darkened and he looked like an octoroon.

'That's annoying . . .' he murmured. 'I was afraid that might happen.'

He stood still for a moment, almost in a trance, then realized he was still holding his toothbrush.

'Hold this,' he said to Colin, shoving it into his hand. 'Sit down, dear,' he said to Chloe.

He walked right the way round his room and then sat down himself.

'Now look,' he said to her, 'you've got something on your lung. Or something *in* your lung, to be more precise. I hoped that it would be . . .'

He stopped and suddenly sprang up.

'Talking about it won't do any good,' he said. 'Come with me. Put that brush down anywhere you like,' he added for Colin's benefit, who really had no idea what to do with it.

Colin wanted to go with Chloe and the professor, but he would have had to sweep aside a kind of heavy but invisible veil which came down between them. His heart struck up an offbeat and strangely anguished rhythm. He used all his might to resist this and, clenching his fists, got hold of himself again. Collecting all his strength together, he managed to take a few steps forward and then, just as he touched Chloe's hand, it disappeared.

She gave her hand to the professor and he led her into a little white room with a chromium ceiling, and the whole of one wall filled by a great shining intricate apparatus.

'I'd prefer it if you sat down,' said the professor. 'It won't take long.'

In front of the machine there was a red silver screen framed in crystal, and a single black control button scintillating like a gem at the base.

'Are you going to wait?' the professor asked Colin.

'If I may,' said Colin.

The professor switched on. The light fled from the room

in a silver stream which shot away under the door and through a ventilating grille just over the machine. Little by little a different kind of light began to glow on the screen.

39

Professor Gnawknuckle tapped Colin on the back.

'Don't worry, my boy,' he said to him. 'It'll be all right.'

Colin looked down, and looked crushed. Chloe was holding his arm. She was making a tremendous effort to appear gay.

'Of course,' she said. 'It won't take long.'

'Sure,' murmured Colin.

'At any rate,' added the professor, 'if she follows my treatment, she'll probably get better.'

'Probably,' said Colin.

They were in the round white waiting-room and Colin's voice echoed back from the ceiling as if it were coming from a great distance.

'In any case,' concluded the professor, 'I'll send you my bill whatever happens.'

'Of course,' said Colin. 'Thank you for everything you've done, doctor . . .'

'And if she doesn't get better,' said the professor, 'you must come back and see me again. If all else fails, there's still an operation – we haven't even mentioned that yet . . .'

'Of course,' said Chloe, pressing Colin's arm. This time she began to sob.

The professor pulled his little beard with both hands.

'It's all very worrying,' he said.

They said nothing for several minutes. A nurse could be seen through the transparent door. She knocked twice, very softly. A green light above the door lit up in front of her and said 'Come In'.

'There's a gentleman asking me to let your visitors know that Nicholas has arrived.'

'Thank you, Nurse Scritch,' said the professor. 'Tell him to wait. They won't be long.' And the nurse went off.

'Well!' murmured Colin, 'then we'll say good-bye to you, doctor . . .'

'Of course . . .' said the professor. 'Good-bye . . . Look after yourselves. See if you can get away for a few weeks . . .'

40

'Wasn't the verdict favourable?' said Nicholas without looking round as he turned the ignition key.

Chloe was still weeping into the white fur and Colin looked dead. The smell of the pavements rose higher and higher. Fumes of ether filled the street.

'Hurry,' said Colin.

'What's wrong with her?' asked Nicholas.

'Oh, things couldn't be worse!' said Colin.

Realizing what he had said he quickly looked at Chloe. He loved her so much – and at that moment he could have killed himself for what he had just said.

Chloe, shrunk in her corner of the car, bit her knuckles. Her shining hair fell into her face and her high heels crushed her fur hat on the seat. She wept furiously, like a baby, but made no noise.

'Forgive me, Chloe darling,' said Colin. 'I'm a brute.'

He shifted up close to her and held her tight. He kissed her poor frightened eyes and felt the muffled beating of her heart inside her chest.

'You're going to get better,' he said. 'What I meant to say was that nothing could be worse than seeing you ill, no matter what the illness might be . . .'

'I'm scared . . .' said Chloe. 'I'm sure he's going to make me have an operation.'

'Of course not,' said Colin. 'You'll be cured long before that.'

'What's wrong with her?' repeated Nicholas. 'Is there anything I can do?'

He too looked very unhappy. His usual self-confidence had been punctured.

'My little Chloe,' said Colin, 'try to calm down.'

'She's bound to be cured in no time,' said Nicholas.

'But this water-lily,' said Colin, 'where could she have caught a thing like that?'

'Water-lily?' queried Nicholas, incredulously.

'She's got one in her right lung,' said Colin. 'At first the professor thought it was only an animal growth. But that's what it is. We saw it on the screen. It's already very large, but it seems we ought to be able to get rid of it.'

'Of course we will,' said Nicholas.

'You can't imagine what it's like,' sobbed Chloe. 'It hurts so much when it moves!'

'Don't cry,' said Nicholas. 'It won't do any good and will only tire you out.'

The car went off. Nicholas drove slowly between the complicated houses. The sun disappeared little by little behind the trees and the wind grew cooler.

'The doctor wants her to go up in the mountains,' said Colin. 'He thinks the cold weather might kill the infection . . .'

'She must have caught it while we were away,' said Nicholas. 'That journey was full of horrible horrors like that . . .'

'He also said that we must keep flowers near her all the time,' added Colin, 'to frighten the one inside . . .'

'Why?' asked Nicholas.

'Because if it blooms,' said Colin, 'it will propagate. But if we don't let it bloom . . .'

'Is that the only treatment?' asked Nicholas.

'No . . .' said Colin.

'What else is there?'

Colin did not answer straight away. He could feel Chloe crying beside him and he hated the torture he was going to have to inflict on her.

'She mustn't have anything to drink . . .' he said.

'What? . . .' said Nicholas. 'Nothing at all?'

'No,' said Colin.

'She can't just drink nothing!'

'Just two spoonfuls a day . . .' murmured Colin.

'Two spoonfuls! . . .' exclaimed Nicholas.

He said nothing more, but stared hard at the road and drove straight ahead.

41

Alyssum rang twice and waited. She thought that the front door seemed narrower than usual. The carpet seemed thin and grey. Nicholas came to the door.

'Hallo! . . .' he said. 'Have you come to see them?'

'Yes,' said Alyssum. 'Are they home?'

'Chloe's here,' said Nicholas. 'Come in.'

He closed the door. Alyssum looked at the carpet.

'It's not as light here as it used to be,' she said. 'What's happening to everything?'

'I don't know,' said Nicholas.

'It's funny,' said Alyssum. 'Didn't there used to be a picture here?'

'I can't really remember . . .' said Nicholas.

He put a thoughtful hand through his hair.

'As a matter of fact,' he said, 'you do get the impression that there's a jinx on things here.'

'Yes,' said Alyssum. 'You certainly do.'

She was wearing a brown suit, very well cut and had a big bunch of jonquils in her hand.

'At any rate,' said Nicholas, *you're* blooming. How're things?'

'Yes, I'm fine,' said Alyssum. 'Chick bought me a suit. Look . . .'

'It suits you,' said Nicholas.

'I'm lucky,' said Alyssum, 'that the Marchioness de Mauvoir is the same size as me. It's second-hand. Chick wanted a scrap of paper that was in one of the pockets, so he bought it for me!'

She looked at Nicholas and added, 'You don't look too well.'

'I wouldn't know,' said Nicholas. 'I feel as if I'm getting old.'

'Let's have a look at your passport,' said Alyssum. He delved into his revolver pocket. 'Here you are,' he said.

Alyssum opened the passport and turned pale. 'How old were you when this was taken?' she asked gravely.

'Twenty-nine . . .' said Nicholas. 'Look . . .'

He counted the wrinkles. There were at least thirty-five. 'I can't understand it . . .' he said.

'It must be a mistake,' said Alyssum, 'because you don't look older than twenty-nine.'

'But I only looked twenty-one then,' said Nicholas.

'We'll soon get it put right for you,' said Alyssum.

'I like your hair,' said Nicholas. 'Come on, come and see Chloe.'

'What's wrong with everything here?' said Alyssum, twice as gravely.

'Oh!' said Nicholas. 'It's her illness. It's affected us all. It will all get put right soon and then I'll grow young again.'

Chloe was lying on the bed, dressed in mauve silk pyjamas with a dressing-gown of pale orange-beige quilted satin. There were lots of flowers all round her, mainly orchids and roses. But there were also hydrangeas, cyclamen, ornettes, baloulettes, rhodridons, camellias, large branches of peach blossom, almond blossom and great armfuls of hibiscus. Her breasts were uncovered and a large blue tendril appeared to be tattooed on the gilded amber skin of the one on the right. Her cheeks were slightly pink, her eyes brilliant but without their old shine, and her hair light and electrified like silken thread.

'You'll catch cold!' said Alyssum. 'Cover yourself up!'

'No,' murmured Chloe. 'I've got to be like that. Doctor's orders!'

'What pretty flowers!' said Alyssum. 'Colin will ruin himself . . .' she added gaily to make Chloe laugh.

'He will,' murmured Chloe. She gave a feeble smile.

'He's looking for a job,' she said in a low voice. 'That's why he isn't here.'

'Why are you talking like that?' asked Alyssum.

'I'm thirsty . . .' said Chloe, breathlessly.

'Do you really only have two spoonfuls a day?' said Alyssum.

'Yes . . .' sighed Chloe.

Alyssum went close and kissed her.

'You'll be better in no time.'

'Yes,' said Chloe. 'I'm going away tomorrow in the car with Nicholas.'

'What about Colin?' asked Alyssum.

'He's got to stay,' said Chloe. 'He's got to work. My poor dear Colin! . . . He's got no doublezoons left . . .'

'Why not?' asked Alyssum.

'The flowers . . .' said Chloe.

'Is it getting bigger?' murmured Alyssum.

'The water-lily?' said Chloe, very quietly. 'No . . . I think it's going away . . .'

'So you're happy then?'

'Yes,' said Chloe. 'But I'm so thirsty.'

'Why don't you put the light on?' asked Alyssum. 'It's dark in here.'

'It's been like it for some time,' said Chloe. 'It's been like it for some time. We can't do anything about it. You try.'

Alyssum went to the switch and a feeble halo wobbled round the bulb.

'The bulbs are dying,' said Chloe. 'The walls are closing in too. And the window in here is shrivelling up!'

'It can't be true,' said Alyssum.

'Just look . . .'

The window which used to run round the whole room now filled no more than a couple of rectangles with very rounded corners. A kind of beanstalk had grown up in the middle, joining top and bottom, and blotting out the sun. The ceiling had very obviously sunk lower and the platform under Colin and Chloe's bed was now only a few inches above the floor.

'How can a thing like this happen?' asked Alyssum.

'I don't know . . .' said Chloe. 'Oh, look, here's a spot of light.'

The mouse with the black whiskers had just come in, carrying a corner broken from one of the kitchen corridor tiles which sent out a brilliant glow.

'When it gets too dark,' explained Chloe, 'it always brings me a little.'

She stroked the little animal who put its loot on the bedside table.

'It's nice of you to come and see me, all the same,' said Chloe.

'Oh,' said Alyssum, 'you know I'm very fond of you.'

'I know,' said Chloe. 'And how's Chick?'

'Oh, fine!' said Alyssum. 'He's bought me a suit.'

'It's pretty,' said Chloe. 'It suits you too.'

She stopped speaking.

'Are you in pain?' said Alyssum. 'You poor darling.'

She went over and put her hand on Chloe's cheek.

'Yes,' groaned Chloe. 'And I'm so thirsty.'

'I know,' said Alyssum. 'If I kissed you, it might quench it a little.'

'Oh, yes,' said Chloe.

Alyssum leaned over her.

Chloe sighed, 'Your lips are so cool . . .'

Alyssum smiled. Her eyes were damp.

'Where are you going?' she asked.

'Not far,' said Chloe. 'Up in the mountains.'

She turned on her left side.

'Do you love Chick very, very much?'

'Yes,' said Alyssum. 'But he loves his books more than me.'

'I'm not sure about that,' said Chloe. 'Maybe it's true. But if I hadn't been married to Colin, then I'd have been so pleased if you could have lived with him.'

Alyssum kissed her again.

42

Chick came out of the shop. There was nothing in there to interest him. He walked along, looking down at his feet in their buffalo-hide shoes, and was surprised to see that one was trying to lead him one way, and the other in the opposite direction. He thought for a few moments, mentally bisected the angle between the two, and set off straight along the line thus produced. He narrowly escaped being run over by a fat greasy taxi and owed his salvation entirely to a graceful leap which landed him right on the feet of a man on the pavement who let out a curse and went straight into hospital to be put together again.

Chick went on his way. There was a bookshop straight ahead. He was in Jimmy Noone Street and the sign was painted in imitation of the one outside Lulu White's Mahogany Hall. He pushed the door, which pushed him equally roughly back, so he went in through the shop-window without any further argument.

The bookseller, perched on top of the complete works of John Galsworthy who had conceived them especially for this purpose, was smoking the pipe of peace. It was a very pretty one made of briar and he was constantly stuffing it with olive leaves. By his side there was also a spittoon for any bait he might swallow, a wet towel for refreshing his temples, and a bottle of Provodka to back up the effects of his smoking.

He gave Chick a smelly disembodied look.

'What do you want?' he asked.

'Just to look at your books . . .' replied Chick.

'Look then,' said the man, and he took aim at the spittoon with his lips – but it was only a false alarm.

Chick went into the bowels of the shop. There was an atmosphere favourable for discovery. He squashed a few insects as he walked farther in. The place smelt of old leather and the smoke of burning olive leaves – which makes a pretty foul stink.

The books were arranged in alphabetical order, but as the bookseller didn't know his alphabet very well, Chick found the Heartre section between T and B. He took out his magnifying glass and started to study the bindings. In a copy of *Breathing and Stuffiness*, the famous critical study of the effects of the common cold, he had soon unearthed a highly interesting fingerprint. Feverishly he took from his coat-pocket a little box in which, besides a camel-hair brush, he kept some fingerprint powder and a copy of *The Model Blood-Hound's Manual* by Cardinal Yesman. He worked with great care, making comparisons with a sheet that he took from his wallet. He stopped, breathless. It was the print of Heartre's left index finger which until then, had never been found by anybody anywhere except on his old pipes.

Clasping the precious find to his heart, he rushed back to the bookseller.

'How much is this?'

The bookseller looked at the book and chuckled. 'So you've found it! . . .'

'What's so extraordinary about it?' asked Chick, pretending he didn't know.

'Ho!' spluttered the bookseller, opening his mouth and letting his pipe fall and fizzle out in the spittoon.

He came out with a forty-four-letter word and rubbed his hands together, delighted that he wouldn't have to suck that unspeakable horror any more.

'I'd like to know . . .' insisted Chick.

His heart almost burst out of his body and began to beat loudly against his ribs with the wild rhythm of jungle drums.

'Now, now, now . . .' said the bookseller, who couldn't stop laughing and was rolling on the floor. 'You're a real jester! . . .'

'Listen,' said Chick, beginning to feel very awkward, 'what are you talking about? . . .'

'When I think,' said the bookseller, 'that to get that fingerprint I had to offer him my pipe of peace half-a-dozen times and learn the same number of conjuring tricks so that I could swop it for another edition when he wasn't looking.'

'Skip it,' said Chick. 'Since you know all about it, how much d'you want for it?'

'It's not very expensive,' said the bookseller, 'but I've got something much better. Wait a moment.'

He got up, disappeared behind a low partition that cut the bookshop in two, scrambled around in something and was back in a flash.

'Here we are,' he said, flinging a pair of trousers on the counter.

'What's this?' gasped Chick, almost afraid of what he might hear.

A delicious thrill ran through his whole body.

'A pair of Heartre's trousers! . . .' announced the bookseller with pride.

'How did you get them?' asked Chick, ecstatic.

'It was while he was giving a lecture . . .' explained the bookseller. 'Never even noticed. There are some holes burnt by his pipe, you know . . .'

'I'll take them,' said Chick.

'What?' asked the bookseller . . . 'Because I've got something else . . .'

Chick put his hand on his chest. It was impossible for him to hold in his heartbeats any longer and he let them out to go crazy for a while.

'Here we are . . .' said the bookseller again.

It was a pipe. On the stem Chick could easily recognize marks made by Heartre's teeth.

'How much?' said Chick.

'You know,' said the bookseller, 'that he's working on an *Encyclopedia of Nausea* in twenty volumes at the moment. I'm going to get the manuscripts . . .'

'But I'll never be able to . . .' said Chick, bumping down to earth again, crushed, dumbfounded and with a sinking heart.

'I couldn't care less about that!' said the bookseller.

'How much for these three?' asked Chick.

'A thousand doublezoons,' said the bookseller, 'and that's my last offer. I refused one thousand two hundred yesterday. I'm only doing this for you because you look as if you'll look after them . . .'

Chick pulled out his wallet. His face was horribly pale.

43

'We've given up using a tablecloth,' said Colin, 'as you can see.'

'I'm not worried about that,' said Chick. 'But I don't understand why the wood has grown all chipped and knotty like that . . .'

'I don't know why it is,' said Colin, dreamily. 'I don't think we know how to clean it properly. It comes from the inside.'

'And wasn't this a woollen carpet before?' asked Chick. 'This one looks as if it's made of cotton . . .'

'It's still the same one,' said Colin. 'I'm *sure* it's not different.'

'It's funny,' said Chick. 'It seems as if the whole world is closing in on you in here!'

Nicholas brought in some greasy soup with chunks of toast submerged in it. He gave them very large helpings.

'What's this, Nicholas?' asked Chick.

'Ockseau with chopped noodles,' replied Nicholas. 'It's smashing!'

'Ah!' said Chick, 'did you get the recipe out of ffroydde?'

'The hell I did!' said Nicholas. 'It came from Joe's, ffroydde may be all right for the snobserver crowd . . . But just look at all the things he expects you to get hold of!'

'But you've got everything you need,' said Chick.

'What?' said Nicholas. 'I've only got the gas and a fridgi-plonk like everyone else. What d'you take us for?'

'Oh . . . Forget it!' said Chick.

He wriggled on his chair. He didn't know how to con-tinue a conversation of that kind.

'Would you like some wine with it?' asked Colin. 'This is all I've got left in the cellar. It's not too bad.'

Chick held out his glass.

'Alyssum came to see Chloe a few days ago,' said Colin, 'but I didn't see her. And yesterday Nicholas took Chloe up into the mountains.'

'Yes,' said Chick. 'Alyssum told me.'

'I had a letter from Professor Gnawknuckle,' said Colin. 'He's asking for loads of money. But I think he's a very good man.'

Colin's head was aching. He had hoped that Chick was going to do all the talking, tell him stories, entertain him. But Chick seemed to be concentrating on something farther away, outside the window. Suddenly he got up and, taking a tape measure from his pocket, went to measure the window-frame.

'I've got a feeling this is changing too,' he said.

'How can it be?' said Colin scornfully.

'It's getting smaller,' said Chick. 'And so is the room . . .'

'What are you talking about?' said Colin. 'That's absolute nonsense . . .'

Chick didn't answer. He took his notebook and pencil and jotted down some figures.

'Did you find a job?' he asked.

'Not yet,' said Colin. 'But I've got an interview later on, and another one tomorrow.'

'What sort of thing are you looking for?' asked Chick. 'Oh, anything!' said Colin. 'So long as I can get some money. Flowers are so expensive.'

'They are,' said Chick.

'How are you getting on at work?' said Colin. 'I got a pal to take over from me,' said Chick, 'because I had so many other things to do . . .'

'Did they take him on?' asked Colin.

'Yes, it all worked out perfectly. He could do my job backwards.'

'So?' asked Colin.

'So when I wanted to go back,' explained Chick, 'they told me my pal was doing fine . . . But, if I wanted a new job, then they'd find something else for me, only the pay wouldn't be so good.'

'Your uncle can't give you anything now,' said Colin.

He did not even make his sentence into a question. It seemed obvious to him.

'It would be rather hard for me to ask him for any,' said Chick. 'He's dead.'

'You never told me . . .'

'It wasn't madly interesting,' murmured Chick.

Nicholas came back again with a greasy pot in which three black sausages were fighting for their lives.

'You'll have to eat them like that,' he said. 'I can't finish them off. They're as hard as old boots and as tough as nails. I put some nitric acid in – that's why they're black – but it wasn't powerful enough to do the trick.'

Colin managed to stick his fork into one of the sausages and it writhed as it gave out an unrhythmical death-rattle.

'I've got one,' he said. 'You have a try, Chick!'

'I am trying,' said Chick, 'but it's not so easy!'

He sent a great splurt of grease flying across the table.

'Hell!' he said.

'Don't worry,' said Nicholas. 'It's good for the woodwork.'

Chick managed to help himself at last, and Nicholas carried away the third sausage on a stretcher.

'I don't know what's going wrong,' said Chick. 'Did it used to be like this here before?'

'No,' confessed Colin. 'Everything everywhere is changing, and I can't do anything to stop it. It's grown like some kind of leprosy since my doublezoons disappeared . . .'

'Haven't you got any left at all?' asked Chick.

'Hardly any,' replied Colin. 'I paid for the mountains in advance and for the flowers too – because I don't want Chloe to go short of anything that might help to get her better. But, apart from that, things aren't too good in themselves.'

Chick had finished his sausage.

'Come and look at the kitchen corridor!' said Colin.

'I'm right behind you,' said Chick.

Through the panes on each side you could just pick out a wan, tarnished sun. Their centres were smothered with black spots. A few skimpy handfuls of rays had got through into the corridor but, as soon as they touched the ceramic tiles that were once so brilliant, they turned to liquid and trickled away into long damp stains. A smell like locked cellars hovered over the walls. In one of the corners the mouse with black whiskers had built a nest on stilts for itself. It could no longer play with the golden rays on the floor like it used to. It was shuddering on a pile of remnants of silk and taffeta, and the damp was causing its long whiskers to cling together. After a supermuscular effort it had managed to scratch some of the tiles to make them shine again, but the task was too mighty for its tiny paws, and now it just stayed in its corner, trembling and worn out.

'Aren't the radiators working?' asked Chick, pulling up the collar of his jacket.

'Of course they are,' said Colin. 'They're switched on all day long, but nothing happens. This is the spot where it all started . . .'

'What a nuisance,' said Chick. 'You ought to get the builders in.'

'They've been,' said Colin, 'and they've been laid up ever since.'

'Oh!' said Chick. 'They'll be all right in a day or two.'

'I don't think so,' said Colin. 'Come on, let's go and finish our lunch with Nicholas.'

They went into the kitchen. There too the room had grown smaller. Nicholas, sitting at a bare little table, was reading a book and munching at something.

'Look here, Nicholas . . .' said Colin.

'All right,' said Nicholas. 'I was just going to bring your afters in.'

'That's not what I meant,' said Colin. 'We're going to eat it here. No, it was something else. Nicholas, you wouldn't like me to give you the sack, would you?'

'Not really,' said Nicholas.

'Well, I think I might have to,' said Colin. 'You're going to seed here. You've grown ten years older in a week.'

'*Seven* years older,' Nicholas corrected him.

'I don't like seeing you like this. It's not doing you any good being here. It's the atmosphere.'

'But it isn't affecting you,' said Nicholas.

'It's not the same for me,' said Colin. 'I've got to get Chloe better and nothing else matters to me, so it doesn't have any effect. How's your club?'

'Never go there these days . . .' said Nicholas.

'I can't take any more of this,' repeated Colin. 'The High-Pottinuices are looking for a cook and I've said you'll go. But first I'd like you to tell me that you'd like to go there.'

'I wouldn't,' said Nicholas.

'Well,' said Colin, 'you're going to go there, whether you like it or not.'

'That's a rotten thing to do to anybody,' said Nicholas. 'I feel like a rat buggering off from the sinking ship.'

'Not at all,' said Colin. 'You *must* go. You know how sad it makes me . . .'

'Yes, I know,' said Nicholas. He closed his book and put down his head in his arms on the table.

'You've got nothing to be sad about,' said Colin.

'I'm *not* sad,' groaned Nicholas.

He looked up. Great tears of silence were in his eyes.

'I'm a nut,' he said.

'You're a great pal, Nicholas,' said Colin.

'No, I'm not,' said Nicholas. 'I'd like to crawl away inside a shell. Then I'd hear nothing but the sea. And nobody would find me and come and disturb me . . .'

44

Colin went up the stairs. They were gloomily lit by un-blinkingly leaden leaded windows. He reached the first floor and found a black door cut into a cold stone wall. Without ringing he went in, filled up a form, gave it to a commissionaire who emptied it, screwed it into a little ball, fed it into the mouth of a ravenous cannon and took careful aim at the inquiry desk in the partition facing him. He ignited the gunpowder, closed his right ear with his left hand, and fired. Then he sat down to recharge his weapon in preparation for the next caller.

Colin stood there until a peal of bells summoned the commissionaire to show him into the chairman's office.

He followed the man along a long winding, rambling passage whose levels went up and down with every step they took. Although the walls were perpendicular to the floors, they twisted and turned with them at each corner, and he had to go at full speed if he wanted to stay upright. Before he knew what had happened, he was standing in front of the chairman's desk. Obediently he sat down in a restive armchair that reared and pranced between his legs and only stood still when its master made an imperative gesture.

'Well? . . .' said the chairman.

'Well. Here I am! . . .' said Colin.

'What do you do?' asked the chairman.

'I've mastered the rudiments . . .' said Colin.

'What I mean,' said the chairman, 'is how do you spend your time?'

'I spend the best part of my time,' said Colin, 'in making things worse.'

'Why?' asked the chairman, in a deteriorated tone.

'Because the best never makes things better,' said Colin.

'Ahem . . . Hum! . . .' murmured the director. 'You know the kind of job we are offering?'

'No,' said Colin.

'Neither do I . . .' said the chairman. 'I'll have to ask my managing director. But you don't look as if you would be suitable . . .'

'Why not?' This time it was Colin who asked the question.

'I don't know . . .' said the chairman.

He seemed nervous and pushed his armchair back a little.

'Don't come any closer! . . .' he snapped.

'But . . . I didn't move . . .' said Colin.

'No . . . No . . .' muttered the chairman. 'That's what they all say . . . And then . . .'

He leaned forward provocatively without taking his eyes off Colin, and picked up his telephone from the desk, shaking it violently.

'Hello! . . .' he shouted. 'Come in here immediately!'

He put back the instrument and continued contemplating Colin suspiciously.

'How old are you?' he asked.

'Twenty-one . . .' said Colin.

'I thought as much . . .' said his interlocutor.

Somebody knocked at the door.

'Come in!' shouted the chairman, and his expression relaxed again.

A man, ravaged by the continual absorption of paper dust and whose bronchia must have been overflowing with reconstituted cellulose paste, came into the room with a file under his arm.

'You've broken a chair,' said the chairman.

'Yes,' said the managing director.

He put the file on the table.

'It can be repaired, you know . . .'

He turned to Colin.

'Do you know how to mend chairs? . . .'

'I think so . . .' said Colin, taken by surprise. 'It isn't very difficult, is it?'

'I've used up three pots of office glue so far,' said the managing director, 'and haven't managed it yet.'

'You'll pay for them,' yelled the chairman. 'I'll deduct the cost of them from your salary . . .'

'I've already taken it from my secretary's,' said the managing director. 'Don't worry, chief.'

'Were you looking for somebody to mend chairs?' asked Colin timidly.

'Of course!' said the chairman. 'We must have been.'

'I don't remember very clearly,' said the managing director. 'But you can't mend a chair . . .'

'Why not?' said Colin.

'Simply because you can't,' said the managing director.

'I wonder how you realized that?' said the chairman.

'Mainly,' said the managing director, 'because these chairs cannot be mended and, in particular, because he doesn't give me the impression of being able to mend a chair.'

'But what has a chair got to do with an office job?' said Colin.

'Do you sit on the floor when you work?' sneered the chairman.

'You can't work very often if you do,' improved the managing director.

'It's perfectly obvious,' said the chairman, 'that you're an idler! . . .'

'That's it . . . An idler . . .' approved the managing director.

'We could never,' concluded the chairman, 'under any circumstances, take on a lazy-bones! . . .'

'Especially when we haven't any work to give him . . .' said the managing director.

'It's absolutely illogical,' said Colin, stunned by their bureaucratic booming.

'Why is it illogical, eh?' asked the chairman.

'Because,' said Colin, 'the last thing you should give an idler to do is work!'

'So that's it,' said the managing director, 'so you want to take over the chairmanship?'

The chairman split his sides laughing at this suggestion.

'He's wonderful . . . !' he said.

His face clouded over and he pushed his armchair still farther back.

'Take him away . . .' he said to the managing director. 'It's clear to me now why he came. Go on, quickly! . . . Buzz off, slacker!' he screamed.

The managing director made a dive for Colin who had smartly grabbed the forgotten file from the table.

'If you lay a hand on me . . .' he threatened.

He backed slowly to the door.

'Clear off!' screeched the chairman. 'Spawndrift of Satan! . . .'

'And you're a silly old bugger,' said Colin, and he turned the handle of the door.

He flung the file at the desk and dashed into the corridor. When he reached the front door the commissionaire fired his cannon at him and the paper bullets made holes in the shape of a skull and crossbones in the upper panel of the door as it swung back.

45

'I can tell that it's a very fine article,' said the junctiquitarian, as he walked round Colin's clavicocktail.

'It's made from genuine crow's-foot maple,' said Colin.

'So I see,' said the junctiquitarian. 'I suppose it works all right?'

'I'm only selling my very best things,' said Colin.

'It must upset you,' said the junctiquitarian, leaning over to examine a little pattern in the grain of the wood.

He blew away a few specks of dust which were spoiling the polish on the piece of furniture.

'Wouldn't you prefer to go out to work for your money and hang on to this? . . .'

Colin remembered the chairman's office and the parting shot and he said 'No.'

'You'll come to it in the end,' said the junctiquitarian, 'when you've got nothing left to sell . . .'

'If my expenses stop rising . . .' said Colin. And he went on . . . 'if my expenses stop growing, then, by selling my things, I should have enough to live on without working. Not live very well, but live all the same.'

'Don't you like work?' asked the junctiquitarian.

'It's horrible,' said Colin. 'It takes a man down to the level of a machine.'

'And your expenses are always going up?' asked the junctiquitarian.

'Flowers are so expensive,' said Colin, 'and so are prices in the mountains too . . .'

'But if she gets better . . .' said the junctiquitarian.

'Ah!' said Colin.

He beamed.

'That would be so marvellous! . . .' he murmured.

'And it's not entirely impossible, is it?' said the junctiquitarian.

'No! Of course not! . . .' said Colin.

'But it will take time,' said the junctiquitarian.

'Yes,' said Colin. 'And the sun is going . . .'

'It will come back,' said the junctiquitarian, encouragingly.

'I don't think so,' said Colin. 'It's moving farther away . . .'
They were quiet for a few moments.

'Is it loaded?' asked the junctiquitarian, pointing to the clavicocktail.

'Yes,' said Colin. 'There's tiger's milk in all its tanks!'

'I'm quite handy on the keyboard. Could we try it out?'

'If you like,' said Colin.

'I'll go and get a chair.'

They were standing in the middle of the shop where Colin had had his clavicocktail taken. All around them there were piles of strange old objects shaped like armchairs, leg-chairs, consoles and heels and other pieces of furniture. It was rather dark and there was a smell of curried polish and blue woodworm. The junctiquitarian took down a horsehair stool with saddle and reins and sat down in front of the clavicocktail. He had put up the *Closed* sign on the door which, being a slave to the truth, had swung shut and ensured that they would not be disturbed.

'Do you know any Duke Ellington? . . .' said Colin.

'Yes,' said the junctiquitarian. 'I'll play "Blues of the Vagabond".'

'How much shall I set it for?' said Colin. 'Three choruses?'

'OK,' said the junctiquitarian.

'Fine,' said Colin. 'That will make gallons. Ready?'

'Perfect,' replied the shopkeeper, and he began to play.

He had a very sensitive touch and the notes flew up, as airborne as the pearls cast from Barney Bigard's clarinet in Duke's version of the tune.

Colin had sat on the floor to listen, with his back against the clavicocktail, and soft paisley-shaped tears slowly came from his eyes, ran down his jacket and trousers and trickled away into the dust. The music passed through him and came out distilled. The result sounded more like 'Chloe' than the 'Blues of the Vagabond'. The junk merchant hummed an accompaniment of pastoral simplicity and swung his head to one side like a rattlesnake. He came to the end of his three choruses and stopped. Colin, filled with contentment to the very bottom of his soul, sat still. It was like the days before Chloe was ill.

'What do you do now?' asked the junctiquitarian . . .

Colin got up and opened the front panel by turning the handle. They took the two glasses that were filled to the brim with shimmering liquid rainbows. The junctiquitarian drank first, licking his lips with his tongue.

'It's got exactly the taste of the blues,' he said. 'And exactly the taste of those blues I've just played. This invention of yours is super! . . .'

'Yes,' said Colin. 'It always did work very well.'

'You know,' said the junctiquitarian, 'I think I'm going to give you an excellent price for it.'

'I'll be very pleased if you do,' said Colin. 'Everything's going very badly for me these days.'

'That's the way things are,' said the junctiquitarian. 'They can't always go well.'

'But they could try not to go badly so frequently,' said Colin. 'We remember good times much better – so what's the good of bad times?'

'Shall I play "Misty Morning"?' suggested the junctiquitarian. 'Does that make a good mixture?'

'Yes,' said Colin. 'It makes something terrific. A pearl-grey mint green cocktail, tasting of peppery smoke.'

The junctiquitarian sat down at the clavikeyboard again and played 'Misty Morning'. Then they drank it. Next he played 'Blue Bubbles' and stopped because he found he was playing two notes at once, and Colin was hearing four different tunes at the same time. Colin carefully put down the lid.

'Well,' said the junctiquitarian, 'shall we talk business now?'

'Yerrup!' said Colin.

'Your clavicocktail is a fantastically gimmicky gadget,' said the junctiquitarian. 'I'll give you three thousand doublezoons for it.'

'Oh, no!' said Colin. 'That's too much.'

'I insist,' said the junctiquitarian.

'But that's idiotic,' said Colin. 'I can't accept it. I'll take two thousand, if you like.'

'No,' said the junctiquitarian. 'Take it back again. I refuse.'

'I can't sell it to you for three thousand,' said Colin. 'That would be daylight robbery! . . .'

'Not at all . . .' insisted the junctiquitarian. 'I know, we'll split it. I'll give you two thousand five hundred doublezoons.'

'All right,' said Colin. 'Done. But how are we going to darn that split?'

'Take your dough . . .' said the junctiquitarian.

Colin took the money and put it neatly in his crocket. He was swaying backwards and forwards.

'I can't stand up straight,' he said.

'Of course you can't,' said the junctiquitarian. 'I hope you'll come and listen to a glass with me now and again?'

'I promise,' said Colin. 'But I must go now, or Nicholas will grumble at me.'

'I'll come part of the way with you,' said the junctiquitarian. 'I've got some shopping to do.'

'That's very kind of you! . . .' said Colin.

They went out of the shop. The green-blue sky was

hanging almost on to the pavement and there were great white patches all over it where the clouds had just burst.

'We've been having some stormy weather,' said the junctiquitarian.

They walked a few yards together and Colin's companion stopped in front of a supermarket.

'Wait for me a moment,' he said. 'I shan't be long.'

He went in. Colin saw him through the window picking up something which he held up to the light and looked at carefully before stuffing it into his pocket.

'Here we are again! . . .' he said, as he closed the door behind him.

'What was it?' asked Colin.

'A spirit level,' replied the junctiquitarian. 'I'm going to play every tune I know once I've taken you home, and after that I'm going for a long, long walk . . .'

46

Nicholas was looking at the stove. He was sitting in front of it with a poker and a blow-lamp and checking up on the inside works. The top of the stove had sunken in and the stout metal sides were growing soft and mouldy like thin slices of gorgonzola. He heard Colin's footsteps in the corridor and looked up. He felt tired. Colin pushed open the door and went in, looking very pleased.

'Well?' asked Nicholas. 'How did you get on?'

'I've sold it,' said Colin. 'Two thousand five hundred . . .'

'Doublezoons? . . .' asked Nicholas.

'Yes,' said Colin.

'Incredible! . . .'

'I wasn't expecting that much either. What were you doing with the stove?'

'Looking it over,' said Nicholas. 'It's trying to turn itself into a camp-fire and cauldron, and I wonder how the hell it's doing it . . .'

'It's odd,' said Colin, 'but no more than the rest. Have you seen the corridor?'

'Yes,' said Nicholas. 'It's like old floorboards now . . .'

'I don't want to have to tell you again,' said Colin, 'that I don't want you to stay here any more.'

'There's a letter,' said Nicholas.

'From Chloe?'

'Yes,' said Nicholas. 'It's on the table.'

As he opened the letter Colin could hear Chloe's silk-soft voice, and he had only to listen to it in order to read the letter. This is what it said,

Colin, my darling,
I am very well and the weather is lovely. The only things I don't like are the snow-moles. They are little animals who burrow their way between the snow and the earth. They have marmalade fur and make lots of noise squeaking in the night. They make big mole-hills out of the snow and everybody trips over them. Everything here is brilliant with sunshine and I'll be back again with you very very soon.

'It's a lovely letter,' said Colin. 'And now, off with you to the High-Pottinuices.'

'I'm not going,' said Nicholas.

'You are,' said Colin. 'They need a cook and I don't want

you here any more . . . You're getting too old, and I told you I've already said you're going!'

'And what about the mouse?' said Nicholas. 'Who'll feed it?'

'I'll look after it,' said Colin.

'You wouldn't know how to,' said Nicholas. 'And if you did that, then how would I know how things were going on?'

'You'd find out,' said Colin. 'The atmosphere here's getting you down. None of you can stand up to it . . .'

'You're always saying that,' said Nicholas, 'and it doesn't explain a thing!'

'Well,' said Colin, 'that isn't the problem! . . .'

Nicholas stood up and stretched. He looked very sad.

'You don't cook anything out of ffroydde any more,' said Colin. 'You neglect the kitchen, and you let yourself go.'

'I don't,' protested Nicholas.

'Let me finish,' said Colin. 'You don't put your best clothes on at the week-end any more, and you don't bother to shave in the mornings.'

'It's not a crime,' said Nicholas.

'It *is* a crime,' said Colin. 'I can't give you as much money as you're worth. But, the way things are going, you're not going to be worth as much as you used to be . . . And it's partly my fault.'

'That's not true,' said Nicholas. 'It's not your fault if you're being messed around.'

'Yes it is,' said Colin. 'It's because I got married and because . . .'

'That's idiotic,' said Nicholas. 'Who'll do the cooking?'

'I will,' said Colin.

'But you'll be working! . . . You won't have the time.'

'No, I won't be working. Don't forget I've sold the clavi-cocktail for two thousand five hundred doublezoons.'

'Yes,' said Nicholas, 'that's put you in front a little.'

'And you're going to the High-Pottinuices,' said Colin.

'Oh!' said Nicholas. 'You get on my nerves. I'll go – but it's a lousy rotten trick.'

'Perhaps you'll get your good manners back again there.'

'You used to complain enough when I did have them . . .'

'Yes,' said Colin, 'because I wasn't worth wasting them on.'

'You make me sick,' said Nicholas. 'You make me sick, sick, and sick . . .'

47

Colin could hear somebody knocking on the front door and he hurried to open it. One of his slippers had a large hole in it so he hid his foot under the carpet.

'You're up in the clouds here,' said Gnawknuckle, going in.

He was puffing and blowing in short pants.

'Good-morning, doctor,' said Colin, blushing because he had to take his foot out from under the carpet.

'You've got a new flat,' said the professor. 'I didn't have to climb so far before.'

'No,' said Colin. 'It's the same.'

'Pull the other one,' said the professor. 'You never let on when you crack a joke so it seems all the funnier in the end.'

'Do I?' said Colin . . . 'Maybe . . .'

'How are things? And how's the patient?' said the professor.

'Getting better,' said Colin. 'She looks better and she's not in pain any more.'

'Hrmm! . . .' said the professor. 'I don't like the sound of that.'

Followed by Colin, he went into Chloe's room and ducked so as not to bang his head against the lintel over the door – but this came down at the same moment and the professor let out an enormous and unconventional Hippocratic oath. From her bed, Chloe laughed when she saw the way the professor was coming in.

The room had grown very small now. Unlike the carpet in the other rooms, it had grown much thicker here and the pile was high. The bed was now in a little alcove with satin curtains. The old big window was perfectly divided into four little square panes by the stalactites and stalagmites whose stony growth was now complete. Everything there was bathed in a greyish – but nevertheless clean – light. And it was warm.

'And you're still telling me that you haven't got a different flat, are you?' said Gnawknuckle.

'I swear to you, doctor . . .' began Colin.

He stopped, because the professor was looking at him in a worried and worrying way.

'. . . I was only joking! . . .' Colin concluded his sentence with an unconvincing laugh.

Gnawknuckle went up to the bed.

'Now,' he said, 'let's have a look at you. I'll have to sound you.'

Chloe opened her swansdown bed-jacket. 'Ah!' said Gnawknuckle. 'That's where they operated on you . . .'

Under her right breast she had a tiny scar, perfectly round.

'Did they pull it out through there when it was dead?' said the professor. 'Was it very long?'

'About a yard, I think,' said Chloe. 'With a great big flower, six inches across.'

'Horrible thing! . . .' mumbled the professor. 'You did have bad luck. They're pretty unusual that large!'

'The other flowers made it die!' said Chloe. 'Especially some vanilla blossom that I had towards the end.'

'Strange,' said the professor. 'I wouldn't have thought vanilla would have had any effect at all. Now juniper or acacia would have been much more likely, in my opinion. But any fool can practise medicine, you know,' he summed up.

'I realize that your guess is as good as mine!' said Chloe.

The professor sounded her. He stood up again.

'Fine,' he said. 'But, of course, you aren't the same as you were before.'

'Aren't I?' said Chloe.

'No,' said the professor. 'One lung has completely collapsed – or almost.'

'I don't care about that,' said Chloe, 'so long as the other one is all right!'

'But if you catch something there,' said the professor, 'it will be rotten for your husband.'

'But not for me?' said Chloe.

'Not for you any more,' said the professor. He stood up.

'I don't want to frighten you for nothing, but do try to be very careful.'

'I am very careful,' said Chloe.

Her eyes grew wide. She put a nervous hand through her hair.

'What must I do to be sure nothing gets in the other one?' she asked, almost with tears in her voice.

'Don't worry, my girl,' said the professor. 'There's no reason why you should catch anything in it.'

He looked round.

'I liked your first flat better. It seemed much more healthy.'

'Yes,' said Colin. 'But it isn't our fault . . .'

'What do you do, my lad?' asked the professor.

'I find things out,' said Colin. 'And I love Chloe.'

'You don't make any money out of your work?' asked the professor.

'No,' said Colin. 'I don't work in the way that people usually understand the expression.'

'Work is a horrible thing. I know only too well,' murmured the professor. 'But if we all did what we liked, nobody would have any money, since . . .'

He stopped himself.

'Last time I was here you showed me a contraption which produced amazing results. Is it still here by any chance?'

'No,' said Colin. 'I've sold it. But I can still give you a drink . . .'

Gnawknuckle stuck his fingers in the collar of his yellow shirt and scratched his neck.

'I'm following you. Good-bye, young lady,' he said.

'Good-bye, doctor,' said Chloe.

She slid down to the foot of the bed and pulled the eiderdown up to her neck. Her face was bright and tender behind the sheets of lavender blue hemmed with purple.

48

Chick went through the turnstile and put his card in the clocking-on machine. As usual, he tripped over the threshold by the iron gates in the passage leading to the workshops, and a violent gust of white steam and black smoke hit him in the face. Noises began to go through his ears. The sinister purring of the main turbo-generators, the hissing and clinking of the rolling ladders on their little herringbone girders joined the roaring wind as it big-dippered over the corrugated iron roofs. The dark passage was lit every six yards by a dull red bulb whose glow trickled lazily over slippery objects and clutched the rugged sides of the walls in order to get round them. Underfoot the pressed steel was warm, though cracked and broken in places, and through the holes one could see the sombre red jaws of the stone furnaces below. Rumbling fluids careered through fat pipes painted in peeling red and grey and, at each beat of the mechanical heart into which the stokers were pumping life, the skeleton of the building bent slightly forward, stood still for thirty seconds and then shuddered from top to toe. Damp drops formed on the walls, sometimes being shaken off by an extra deep throb. When one of these drops fell on to his neck, Chick shivered. The water was rusty, and smelt of ozone. The passage took a sharp turn to the right at the end and the floor here was completely transparent, looking over the workshops.

Down below, in front of each mammoth machine, a man was struggling, struggling so as not to be slashed and torn apart by the voracious cogs facing him. Every man's right foot was held down by a heavy iron ring. They were only let off twice a day – at night and at noon. They were fighting with the machines for the pieces of metal which came clashing out of the narrow orifices in their tops. If they weren't picked up in time, the pieces fell back almost immediately into the fierce mouths swarming with gnashing cogs where they were ground down again.

There were all shapes and sizes of apparatus. Chick was accustomed to the scene. He worked at the end of one of the workshops and had to make sure that the machines were in good working order and instruct the men to repair them when they jammed after having wrenched off a tough limb or stringy piece of flesh from one of them.

Long sprays, shimmering with reflections, crossed the area diagonally to purify the air. The smoke, metal dust and warm oil condensed around these sprays and rose in tall thin columns above each machine. Chick looked up. The pipes were still going along with him. He reached the cage of the descending platform, went in and closed the door behind him. He took one of Heartre's books from his pocket, pressed the button, and read as much as he could before he reached the bottom.

The platform landed on the metal buffer with a dull thud and wrenched him from his reverie. He stepped out and went to his office. It was a feebly lit glass box from which he could see across the workshops. He sat down, opened his book again, and went on reading from where he had left off and was soon gently lulled to sleep by the throbbing fluids in the pipes and the noises of the machines.

A discordant note in the midst of the hubbub made him suddenly open his eyes and look up. He looked round to see where the odd note might be coming from. One of the purifying sprays had stopped dead in the middle of the shed and stayed rigid in the air as if it had been cut in two.

The four machines which it had stopped serving began to quake. From afar you could see them slowing down and a vague silhouette sink before each of them. Chick put down his book and rushed out. He ran to the board that controlled the sprays and hurriedly pulled a lever. The broken spray did not move. It was like the blade of a severed scimitar. The smoke from the four machines curled in the air like rival whirlwinds. He left the control-board and rushed over to the machines which were slowly running down. Their operators were lying on the ground, their right legs bent under them at an awkward angle because of the iron rings, and their four right hands were sliced off at the wrists. Their blood boiled as it spilt on the metal of the chain and a horrible smell of burning living flesh spread across the shed.

Chick unlocked the rings holding the bodies down with his key, and stretched them out in front of their machines. Then he went back to his office and ordered the duty stretcher-bearers over the phone. Then he went straight back to the control-board to try to get the spray working again. There was nothing doing. The liquid shot straight out but, when it reached the position of the fourth machine, it simply disappeared. The break in the spray was neat and clean as if it had been chopped through by an axe.

Annoyed, and feeling in his pocket to make sure that his book was there, he went off to the main office block. As he left the workshop he stood aside to let the stretcher-bearers pass with the four bodies that they had piled on to a little electric trolley ready to dump them into the main sewer.

He took a different corridor. Far ahead of him the little trolley skidded and turned with a dull hum, sending out occasional sparks. The low ceiling reverberated with the sound of his footsteps on the metal floor. The floor began to slope upwards slightly. In order to get to the main office block he had to go through three other workshops and Chick meandered along his way. At last he reached the main block and went into the personnel officer's department.

'There's been some damage to numbers seven hundred and nine, ten, eleven and twelve,' he told a secretary behind a desk. 'There are four men to be replaced and I think their machines will have to be scrapped. Can I have a word with the personnel officer?'

The secretary pressed a few red buttons on a varnished mahogany board and said 'Go in. He's expecting you.'

Chick went in and sat down. The personnel officer gave him a puzzled look.

'I need four men,' said Chick.

'OK,' said the personnel officer, 'you can have them in the morning.'

'One of the purification sprays has stopped working,' he said.

'Nothing to do with me,' said the personnel officer. 'Go next door.'

Chick went out and through the same formalities before going into the chief engineer's office.

'One of the purification sprays has broken down,' he said.

'Altogether?'

'It won't reach to the end,' said Chick.

'Couldn't you repair it?'

'No,' said Chick. 'There's nothing doing.'

'I'll get your workshop looked over,' said the chief engineer.

'Hurry,' said Chick. 'My production's going down while I wait.'

'That's nothing to do with me,' said the chief engineer. 'See the production manager about that.'

Chick reached the next block and went in to see the production manager. The office there was brilliantly lit and on the wall behind the desk a red line, like a caterpillar on a leaf, was slowly crawling upwards to the right of a large matt glass panel. Underneath the chart the needles on large circular indicators were going round even more slowly under their chrome-edged glasses.

'Your production's gone down by seven per cent,' said the production manager. 'What's wrong?'

'Four machines out of order,' said Chick.

'When it reaches eight per cent you get your cards,' said the production manager.

He swung round on his chromium chair and looked at the indicator.

'Seven point eight per cent,' he said. 'In your shoes I'd have started getting my things ready.'

'It's the first time anything like this has happened to me,' said Chick.

'I'm sorry,' said the production manager. 'Perhaps we could transfer you to another shift . . .'

'I'm not very keen on that,' said Chick. 'I'm not even very keen on work. It's not my favourite pastime.'

'Nobody has the right to say that,' said the production manager. 'You're fired,' he added.

'I couldn't help it,' said Chick. 'Where's your sense of justice?'

'Never heard of it,' said the production manager. 'Anyway, I'm too busy to waste my time talking to you.'

Chick went out of the office. He went back to see the personnel officer.

'Can I have my money?' he asked.

'Number?' said the personnel officer.

'Workshop 700. Engineer.'

'Just a minute.'

He turned to his secretary and said, 'Do the necessary.'

Then he spoke into an internal speaker.

'Hello!' he said. 'Send a replacement engineer, type 5, to Workshop 700.'

'Here you are,' said the secretary, handing an envelope to Chick. 'A hundred and ten doublezoons.'

'Thank you!' said Chick, and he went out. He bumped into a tired-looking, thin, fair, young man. This was the engineer who was going to replace him. Chick went to the nearest lift and stepped into the car.

49

'Come in,' said the record-maker.

He looked up at the door. It was Chick.

'Good-morning,' said Chick. 'I've come to collect those recordings I brought in.'

'I'm just doing your account,' said the record-maker. 'For cutting thirty sides, making special tools, engraving twenty numbered copies by pantograph on each side . . . I make it that you owe us a hundred and eight doublezoons in all. I'll let you have the discs for a hundred and five.'

'Here you are,' said Chick. 'I've got a cheque for a hundred and ten doublezoons – I'll endorse it and you can give me back five doublezoons in cash.'

'Agreed,' said the record-maker.

He pulled out his drawer and gave Chick a brand new five-doublezoon note.

The flames in Chick's eyes – that were the light of his face – flickered out.

50

Isis got out. Nicholas was driving the car. He looked at his watch and followed her with his eyes as she went into Colin and Chloe's house. He had a new white gaberdine uniform and a white leather cap with a peak. He had grown young again, but some deep inner disturbance showed through the lines of worry in his expression.

The width of the stairs suddenly diminished when they reached Colin's floor and Isis could touch the banisters and the cold wall at the same time without putting out her arms. The carpet was nothing more than a thin fluff which hardly covered the boards. She reached the landing, slightly out of breath, and rang.

Nobody came to open the door. There was no sound on the staircase, apart from an occasional creak followed by a plop every time a tread gave way.

Isis rang again. On the other side of the door she could hear the tiny trill of the little steel hammer on the metal bell. She gave the door a push and it burst open.

She went in and tripped over Colin. He was stretched out on the floor with his arms straight out . . . His eyes were closed. It was dark in the doorway. A halo of light could be seen round the window, but it did not come in. He was breathing quietly. He was asleep.

Isis bent down, knelt by his side and touched his cheek. His skin trembled a little and his eyes moved beneath their lids. He looked at Isis and seemed to fall asleep again. Isis gave him a little shake. He sat up, put his hand over his mouth, and yawned. 'I was asleep.'

'So I see,' said Isis. 'Don't you sleep in bed any more?'

'No,' said Colin. 'I wanted to stay here and wait for the doctor, then go and fetch some flowers.'

He seemed to have no clear idea of what he was doing.

'What's the trouble?' said Isis.

'It's Chloe,' said Colin. 'She's started coughing again.'

'It's probably a little irritation still there,' said Isis.

'No,' said Colin. 'It's the other lung.'

Isis got up and ran into Chloe's bedroom. The parquet floor squelched under her feet. The room was unrecognizable. Chloe was in bed, her head half hidden in the pillow, coughing silently but without stopping. She pulled herself up slightly when she heard Isis come in, and took a deep breath. She put on a feeble little smile as Isis drew near, sat on the bed and took her in her arms like a sick baby.

'Don't cough, Chloe darling,' murmured Isis.

'What a pretty flower you're wearing,' whispered Chloe, breathing deeply the perfume of the big red carnation pinned in Isis's hair. 'That's done me good,' she added.

'Are you ill again?' said Isis.

'It's the other lung, I think,' said Chloe.

'No,' said Isis. 'It's the first one that's still making you cough a little.'

'No,' said Chloe. 'Where's Colin? Has he gone to get me some flowers?'

'He won't be long,' said Isis. 'I bumped into him. Has he got any money?' she added.

'Yes,' said Chloe, 'he's still got some left. But it doesn't do any good. It doesn't stop anything! . . .'

'Are you in pain?' asked Isis.

'Yes,' said Chloe, 'but not a lot. The room has changed. Look.'

'I like it better this way,' said Isis. 'It was too big before.'

'What are the other rooms like?' said Chloe.

'Oh . . . Fine . . .' said Isis, evasively.

She could still remember the sensation of the parquet as cold and icy as a forgotten swamp.

'I don't care if it all changes,' said Chloe, 'so long as it's warm and comfortable . . .'

'Sure!' said Isis. 'A small flat's much cosier.'

'The mouse stays with me,' said Chloe. 'You can see it there in the corner. I don't know what it's doing. It didn't want to go into the corridor.'

'Mm . . .' said Isis.

'Let me smell your carnation again,' said Chloe. 'It made me feel so good.'

Isis unpinned it from her hair and gave it to Chloe who put it to her lips and breathed in deeply.

'How is Nicholas?' she said.

'Fine,' said Isis. 'But he isn't cheerful like he used to be. I'll bring you some more flowers when I come back.'

'I was very fond of Nicholas,' said Chloe. 'Aren't you going to marry him?'

'I can't,' murmured Isis. 'I'm far beneath him . . .'

'That doesn't matter,' said Chloe, 'if he loves you . . .'

'My parents wouldn't dare suggest it to him,' said Isis. 'Oh! . . .'

The carnation suddenly went pale, crumpled up and seemed to wither and desiccate. Then it fell on to Chloe's chest in a fine powder.

It was Chloe's turn to say '*Oh*' this time. 'I'm going to start coughing again!' she said. 'Did you see that? . . .'

She stopped to put her hand to her mouth. A violent fit of coughing overcame her again.

'It's . . . this awful thing that I've got . . . it makes them all die . . .' she babbled.

'Don't talk,' said Isis. 'It's not important. Colin is bringing you some more back.'

The light in the bedroom was blue, and in the corners it was almost green. There were no signs of dampness yet, and the pile on the carpet was still fairly high, but one of the four square windows had almost completely closed.

Isis heard Colin's damp footsteps at the door.

'Here he is,' she said. 'He's sure to have some for you.'

Colin came in. He had an enormous bunch of lilac in his arms.

'Here you are, Chloe darling,' he said. 'Take them! . . .'

She held out her arms.

'You're so kind, my darling,' she said.

She put the flowers down on the other pillow, turned on her side and buried her face in the sweet white blooms.

Isis stood up.

'Are you going?' said Colin.

'Yes,' said Isis. 'Somebody's waiting for me. Next time I come I'll bring some more flowers.'

'Could you be nice and kind and come tomorrow morning?' said Colin. 'I've got to go and look for a job and I don't want to leave her all alone until the doctor's seen her.'

'I'll be here . . .' said Isis.

She bent down, very carefully, and kissed Chloe on her soft cheek. Chloe put her hand up and touched Isis's face, but she did not look round. She was greedily breathing the scent of the lilac which was coiling round her gleaming hair in slow spirals.

51

Colin made his way painfully along the road. It sloped down sideways between the piles of earth. The glass domes rising above them took on a misty sea-green bloom in the light of dawn.

Now and again he would look up and read the signs to reassure himself that he had taken the right direction. Then he saw the sky, streaked horizontally with dirty brown and blue.

Far ahead of him, above the shallow embankments, he could see the rows of chimneys belonging to the main hothouse.

In his pocket he had the newspaper in which they were asking for men from twenty to thirty to help prepare the country's defences. He was walking as quickly as he could, but his feet sank into the warm earth into which the surrounding buildings and the road appeared to be sinking too. There were no plants to be seen. There was nothing but earth, earth that had been rapidly heaped up into roughly similar blocks on all sides to form shaky embankments. Sometimes a heavy mass of earth would break loose, roll all the way down the slope and squash itself flat on the surface of the road.

In certain places the embankments were very low and through the cloudy panes of the domes Colin could pick out dark blue figures moving about like silhouettes.

He stepped out quicker, wrenching his feet up from the holes they were making in the muddy earth. The earth was sucked straight back into them and soon all that was left was a sort of shallow dimple that could hardly be noticed. And then that disappeared almost immediately.

The chimneys were getting nearer. Colin felt his heart turning about inside his chest like a savage beast. He held tightly on to his newspaper through the material of his pocket.

The slippery earth fell away under his feet, but he seemed to sink in less and the road grew noticeably firmer. He noticed that the first chimney was quite near him, stuck into the earth like a post. Dark birds flew round the top of it from which thin green smoke was coming. A rounded mound at the base of the chimney prevented it falling over. The buildings began a little farther on. There was only one door.

He went in, scraped his feet on a shining mesh of keen blades, and followed a low corridor that was throbbing with flickering lights. It was paved with red brick, and the upper parts of the walls, like the ceiling, were made of glass bricks, several inches thick, through which dark motionless shapes could be glimpsed indirectly. Right at the end of the corridor there was a door. The number mentioned in the paper was on it, and Colin went in without knocking as he had been instructed to do in the advertisement.

An old man in a white overall, with close-cropped hair, was reading an official manual behind his desk. All kinds of arms were hanging from the wall – crystal field-glasses, flame-rifles, death-throwers, and a complete collection of every shape and size of heart-snatcher.

'Good-morning, sir,' said Colin.

'Good-morning, sir,' said the man.

His voice was cracked and worn with age.

'I've come about the advertisement,' said Colin.

'Have you?' said the man. 'You're the first to apply for a month. It's fairly hard work, you know . . .'

'Maybe,' said Colin, 'but the pay is good!'

'Dithering Deities!' said the man. 'It'll wear you out, I'm telling you. And maybe the money isn't very good when you consider the amount of work you have to do for it. But there, it isn't my place to run down the way they do things here. And you can see I'm still alive . . .'

'Have you been here long?' said Colin.

'A year,' said the man. 'I'm twenty-nine.'

He passed a shaking wrinkled hand across the lines of his face.

'But now I've made a success of it, you see . . . I can sit in my office all day and read the rules and regulations . . .'

'I need money,' said Colin.

'People often do,' said the man. 'But work turns you into a philosopher. After a few months you'll find you didn't need it so badly after all.'

'It's to help cure my wife,' said Colin.

'Oh . . . Indeed?' said the man.

'She's ill,' explained Colin. 'I'm not keen on work.'

'In that case, I'm sorry for you,' said the man. 'When a woman is ill, she's no good for anything any more.'

'I love her,' said Colin.

'No doubt,' said the man, 'otherwise you wouldn't want to work so badly. I'll show you what your job is. It's on the next floor up.'

He guided Colin through immaculate passages with very low vaulted roofs and up red brick staircases until they came to a door, with others on either side of it, which had a symbol marked on it.

'Here you are,' said the man. 'Go in and I'll tell you what to do.'

Colin went in. The room was square and tiny, and the walls and the floor were made of glass. On the floor was a large heap of earth shaped like a rough coffin, but about a yard deep. A thick woollen blanket was rolled up beside it on the floor. No furniture. A little shelf let into the wall held a blue iron casket. The man went over to it and opened it. He took out a dozen shining cylindrical objects with minute holes in the middle.

'This earth is sterile. You know what that means,' said the man. 'We need first class material to defend the country. To grow straight, undistorted rifle barrels we came to the conclusion, some time ago, that we needed human warmth. That's true, anyway, for every kind of arms.'

'Yes,' said Colin.

'Now you have to make a dozen little holes in the earth,' said the man, 'where your heart and liver come. Then you stretch out on the earth after you've stripped. Cover yourself with that sterilized blanket, and do your best to give out a perfectly regular heat.'

He gave a crackly laugh and smacked his right thigh.

'I made fourteen a day the first three weeks of every month when I first came. Ah . . . I was tough! . . .'

'And then?' said Colin.

'Then you stay like that for twenty-four hours. At the end of the twenty-four hours the barrels should have grown. Somebody will come and take them away. The earth is watered with oil, and you start all over again.'

'Do they grow downwards?' said Colin.

'Yes. The light comes from underneath,' said the man.
'Their phototropism is positive, but they grow downwards
because they are heavier than the earth. We specially put
the light underneath so that they won't grow distorted.'

'How about the bore?' said Colin.

'This species grow ready-bored,' said the man. 'They're
tested seeds.'

'What are the chimneys for?' asked Colin.

'They're for ventilation,' said the man. 'And for steriliz-
ing the blankets and the buildings. It's not worth taking
special precautions because it's all done very energetically.'

'Wouldn't it work with artificial heat?' said Colin.

'Not very well,' said the man. 'They need human warmth
to grow to the right size.'

'Do women work here?' said Colin.

'They couldn't do this work,' said the man. 'Their chests
aren't flat enough for the heat to be evenly enough distrib-
uted. Now I'll let you get on with it.'

'Will I really get ten doublezoons a day?' said Colin.

'You will,' said the man, 'and a bonus if you make more
than twelve barrels a day . . .'

He went out of the room and closed the door. Colin
looked at the twelve seeds in his hand. He put them down
and began to take off his clothes. His eyes were closed, and
every so often his lips trembled.

52

'I don't know what's happening,' said the man. 'You started off so well. But we can only make special arms with these latest ones.'

'You're still going to pay me?' said Colin, worried.

He should have been taking home seventy double-zoons with ten doublezoons bonus. He had been doing his very best, but the barrel inspections had shown several anomalies.

'See for yourself,' said the man.

He picked up one of the barrels and showed Colin the funnel-shaped end.

'I can't understand it,' said Colin. 'The first ones were perfectly cylindrical.'

'Of course we can make blunderbusses out of them,' said the man, 'but we gave up using them five wars ago and we've already got a large surplus stock. It's all very annoying.'

'I'm doing my best,' said Colin.

'Of course you are,' said the man. 'You'll get your eighty doublezoons.'

He took a sealed envelope from his desk drawer.

'I had it brought here to save you going to the pay office,' he said. 'Sometimes it takes months to get your money – and you seem to need it quickly.'

'Thanks very much,' said Colin.

'I haven't gone through the ones you made yesterday yet,' said the man. 'They'll bring them in presently. Would you mind waiting for a moment?'

His rasping, croaking voice hurt Colin's ears as it went in.

'I'll wait,' he said.

'You see,' said the man, 'we're forced to pay very strict attention to these details because one rifle must be exactly the same as another, even if we haven't got any cartridges . . .'

'Yes . . .' said Colin.

'We don't often have any cartridges,' said the man. 'They're behind on the cartridge schedules. We've got large stocks for a model we don't make any more, but we haven't been told to make any for the new rifles, so we can't use them. Anyway, it doesn't matter much. What's the good of a rifle against a fodder cannon? The enemies make one fodder cannon for every two of our rifles. So at least we have superiority of numbers. But a fodder cannon isn't going to be scared by a couple of rifles, especially if they've got no ammunition . . .'

'Don't we make fodder cannons here?' asked Colin.

'We do,' said the man, 'but we've only just completed our programme for the last war. So of course they don't work very well and have to be scrapped. As they're very strongly made it's taking us quite a time.'

There was a knock on the door and the quartermaster appeared, pushing a white sterilized trolley. Under a white cloth there was a slight bulge. This wouldn't have happened with strictly cylindrical barrels and Colin felt very worried. The quartermaster went out and closed the door.

'Ah! . . .' said the man. 'It still doesn't look as if they're right.'

He lifted the cloth. There were twelve cold blue steel barrels – and, at the end of each, a beautiful white rose was in full bloom, with drops of dew and beige shadows in the curves of its velvety petals.

'Oh! . . .' gasped Colin. 'Aren't they lovely! . . .'

The man said nothing. But he coughed twice.

'There'll be no point in you coming back tomorrow,' he said after a moment's hesitation.

His fingers touched the end of the trolley nervously.

'Can I take them for Chloe?' said Colin.

'They'll die,' said the man, 'if you pluck them from the steel. They're made of steel too, you know . . .'

'They can't be . . .' said Colin.

He delicately touched one of the roses and tried to snap its stem. His finger slipped and one of the petals made a cut several inches long in his hand. His hand began to bleed and he put it to his mouth to stick the dark blood that began to pulse out. He looked at the red curve on the white petal. The man tapped him on the shoulder and gently showed him the door.

53

Chloe was asleep. During the day the water-lily let her borrow the beautiful creamy colour of its flesh, but while she slept it was hardly worth while, and the pink flushed back into her cheeks. Her eyes made two blue stains below her hazy brows, and from a distance it was impossible to tell whether they were open or shut. Colin was sitting waiting on a chair in the dining-room. Chloe was surrounded by many different kinds of flowers. He could spare an hour or two before going to look for another job. He wanted to take a rest so that he could make a good impression and get something really remunerative. It was almost dark in the room. The window was now only three inches above the sill and the light crept in through a narrow slit. It fell just on his eyes and forehead. The rest of his face remained in shadow. The record-player no longer worked. Now it had to be wound up for every record and that tired him out. The records were wearing out too. You could hardly recognize the tunes on some of them. If Chloe needed something, he knew that the mouse would come and tell him straight away. Was Nicholas going to marry Isis? What kind of dress would she wear for her wedding? Who was ringing at the door?

'Hello, Alyssum,' said Colin. 'Have you come to see Chloe?'

'No,' said Alyssum. 'I've just come.'

They might as well stay in the dining-room. Alyssum's hair made it lighter there. And there were two chairs left.

'Were you fed up?' said Colin. 'I know what it can be like.'

'I've left Chick there,' said Alyssum. 'At home. He's all right.'

'You must have something to tell me,' said Colin.

'No,' said Alyssum. 'I've got to find somewhere else to stay.'

'Oh, yes,' said Colin. 'He's redecorating . . .'

'No,' said Alyssum. 'He's got all his books all round him, but he doesn't want me any more.'

'Did you have a row?' said Colin.

'No,' said Alyssum.

'He just misunderstood what you said to him. But when he's calmed down you can talk it all over with him.'

'He simply told me that he had just enough doublezoons to get his latest book bound in nulskin,' said Alyssum, 'and he couldn't bear to keep me with him because he had nothing to give me and I'd grow old and ugly wearing my hands out.'

'Of course he's right,' said Colin. 'You mustn't go out to work.'

'But I love Chick,' said Alyssum. 'I'd have worn my fingers to the bone for him.'

'That wouldn't do any good,' said Colin. 'Nobody would allow you to – you're too pretty.'

'Why did he kick me out?' said Alyssum. 'Did I really use to be very pretty?'

'I don't remember,' said Colin. 'But I know that I'm very fond of your hair, your face and your figure.'

'Look,' said Alyssum.

She stood up, pulled the little ring at the top of her zip, and her dress fell to the ground. It was a light woollen dress.

'Mmmm . . .' said Colin.

It became very light in the room and Colin could see every inch of Alyssum. Her breasts seemed ready to take off, and the calves and thighs of her long nimble legs were firm and warm to the touch.

'Is one allowed to kiss?' said Colin.

'Yes,' said Alyssum. 'I'm very fond of you too.'

'You'll catch cold,' said Colin.

She went close to him. She sat on his knees and tears began to stream silently from her eyes.

'Why doesn't he want me any more?'

Colin gently cuddled her.

'He doesn't understand. You know, Alyssum, he's a good kid, all the same . . .'

'He used to love me lots,' said Alyssum. 'He thought his

books would be willing to share him with me! But that's impossible.'

'You'll catch cold,' said Colin.

He kissed her and stroked her hair.

'Why didn't I meet you first?' said Alyssum. 'I'd have given you just as much love – but I can't now. It's him I love.'

'I know that,' said Colin. 'I love Chloe more than anyone now, too.'

He made her stand up and picked up her dress.

'Put it on again, pet,' he said. 'You'll catch cold.'

'I won't,' said Alyssum. 'And it wouldn't matter if I did.'

And she put on her dress again as if in a dream.

'I don't like the idea of you being sad,' said Colin.

'You're sweet,' said Alyssum, 'but I *am* very sad. I think there might still be something I could do for Chick, all the same.'

'Go home and see your parents,' said Colin. 'They're bound to be pleased to see you . . . Or go and see Isis.'

'Chick won't be there,' said Alyssum. 'And I don't want to be anywhere if Chick isn't there too.'

'He'll come,' said Colin. 'I'll go and see him.'

'Don't,' said Alyssum. 'You won't be able to get in. He always locks the door.'

'I'll see him all the same,' said Colin. 'If not, then he'll come round to see me.'

'I don't think so,' said Alyssum. 'It's not the same Chick any more.'

'Of course it is,' said Colin. 'People don't change, only things!'

'I don't know,' said Alyssum.

'I'll come with you,' said Colin. 'I've got to go out and look for a job.'

'I'm not going that way,' said Alyssum.

'Then I'll come down the stairs with you,' said Colin.

She was standing in front of him. He put his two hands on her shoulders. He could feel her warm neck and her soft curling hair close to his skin. He followed the outline of her body with his hands. She had stopped weeping. She did not seem to be there at all.

'I don't want you to do anything stupid,' said Colin.

'Don't worry,' said Alyssum. 'I won't . . .'

'Come and see me again,' said Colin, 'next time you're fed up . . .'

'Perhaps I'll take you up on that,' said Alyssum.

She looked farther inside the flat. Colin took her hand. They went down the stairs. Every so often they slipped on the damp treads. At the bottom Colin said good-bye to her. She stood and watched him go.

54

The latest one was just back from the binder's and Chick lovingly stroked it before putting it back in its wrapping. It was bound in rich green nulskin with the name Heartre deeply and blindly tooled into the spine. On one shelf Chick had the whole of the ordinary edition of his works. The variants, manuscripts, proofs and special pages occupied various niches set into the wall.

Chick sighed. Alyssum had left him that morning. He had to tell her to go. All he had left was one doublezoon and a piece of cheese. Her dresses in the wardrobe were getting in the way of Heartre's old clothes that his bookseller could always work miracles and get for him. He couldn't remember the last time he had kissed her. His time was too precious to be wasted on kissing her. His record-player had had to be mended so that he could learn Heartre's lectures by heart. If the records should get broken, then the words would still be preserved.

Every one of Heartre's books was there – every one of his published works. There were luxurious bindings, books carefully protected by leather cases, golden toolings, precious editions with wide blue margins, limited printings on fly-paper and others on blank partridge or rice caper. A complete wall was reserved for them, honeycombed into cute little pigeon-holes lined with genuine high-quality suede. Each work occupied one pigeon-hole. On the wall opposite, arranged in paperback piles, were Heartre's articles and interviews, all fervently snipped from magazines, newspapers and the innumerable periodicals that he deigned to favour with his prolific collaboration.

Chick put his hand to his forehead. How long had Alyssum been living with him? . . . Colin's doublezoons were supposed to have helped him to marry her – but she wasn't all that worried about getting married. She was content to wait – happy simply to be with him – but you can't accept things like that from a woman – things like staying with you simply because she loves you. He loved her too. But how could he let her waste her time like that – especially now that she had given up her interest in Heartre . . . How could anyone fail to be interested in a man like Heartre? . . . A man capable of writing – and with what clarity! – anything on any subject whatsoever . . . Surely it would take Heartre less than a year to complete his *Encyclopedia of Nausea*. The Marchioness de Mauvoir would collaborate with him on this – and there would be some fabulous manuscripts. But between now and then he would have to find and save enough doublezoons to keep an account going with the bookseller. Chick hadn't paid his income tax. But what he would have given them was much more useful to him in the form of a copy of *We Always Closed Our Zips*. Alyssum *would* have preferred Chick to use his doublezoons to pay his taxes, and had even suggested selling some of her own things so that he could do this. He'd said *yes*, and it had come to exactly the right price for binding *We Always Closed Our Zips*. Alyssum managed very well without her pearls.

He wondered whether to unlock the door again. She might be waiting behind it, listening for him to turn the key. But he didn't think so. Her footsteps on the stairs echoed away like a woodpecker falling asleep. She could easily go back home to her parents and pick up her studies where she had left off. After all, she wouldn't be far behind the others on her course . . . It's easy to catch up on missed lectures . . . But Alyssum hadn't done any work at all lately. She'd been too interested in Chick – in cooking things for him and ironing his tie. The taxes could be forgotten. Nobody's ever heard of people coming to chase you out of your home because you haven't paid your taxes! No, things like that don't happen. You can give them a doublezoon on account, and then they leave you alone for a few more years. Does a man like Heartre bother to pay his taxes? He probably does – yet, after all, should one, from the moral point of view, pay one's taxes so that, in return, one can have the right to be locked up because other people pay theirs to feed the police and senior civil servants? It's a vicious circle that's got to be broken – nobody should pay any more for a long, long time, and then all the collectors would die of consumption and there'd be no more wars.

Chick lifted the lid of his double-turntabled record-player and put on two different Jean Pulse Heartre records. He wanted to listen to them both at the same time so that new ideas could spring from the meeting of two old ones. He placed himself equidistantly between the two loud-speakers so that his head would be just at the spot where the idea barrier would break. Then he could automatically preserve the results of the impact.

The needles spat on the ends of the tails of the hollow snails, lodged themselves into the depths of the grooves, and Heartre's double words began to ring through Chick's brain. Sitting in his chair he looked out of the window and noticed smoke rising here and there above the roofs in huge blue spirals. Their undersides were red, as if it were the smoke from paper burning. He watched the red slowly but surely take over from the blue. The stereophonic collision of words in his head coincided with great flashes of light, opening up a field of repose to his deep fatigue that was like lush and new-mown moss in May.

55

The police commissergeant pulled his whistle from his pocket and used it to strike an enormous Peruvian gong which was hanging behind him. Tipped boots could be heard galloping across the floors above, followed by continuous crashes, and six of his best men-at-arms tobogganed down the pole and burst into his office.

They got up, smacked their backsides to get rid of the dust, sprang to attention and saluted.

'Douglas!' called the commissergeant.

'Present!' replied the first man-at-arms.

'Douglas!' repeated the commissergeant.

'Present!' replied the second.

And so the roll-call went on. The police commissergeant could hardly be expected to remember the first name of every man, and Douglas was a traditional and conventional enough overture for most of them.

'Special mission!' he ordered.

As one man, the six men-at-arms slapped their hands on their puttock bockets to show that they were equipped with their twelve-squirter equalizers.

'And I personally am in command!' emphasized the commissergeant.

He thumped on the gong with violence. The door opened and a secretary appeared.

'I'm off,' announced the commissergeant. 'Special mission. Shorthandify please!'

The secretary took up her shorthand pad and pencil and crossed her legs in official taking-down position number six.

'Collection of overdue taxes from Chick Esquire, following seizure of coinage,' dictated her chief. 'Smuggling contraband tobacco with serious indictment. Total, or at least partial, confiscation of goods, aggravated by breaking up of happy home.'

'Got it!' said the secretary.

'On our way!' ordered the police commissergeant. 'Quick march!'

He stood up and went to the head of the squad whose

twelve feet took off in a clumsy imitation of the flight of the waffle-cuckoo. The men were dressed in skin-tight black leather with silver breast-plates and head-hugging helmets of blackened steel, which went right down over the napes of their necks and protected their foreheads and temples. They all wore heavily tipped boots. The commissergeant wore similar gear, but in red leather, and two golden stars twinkled on each of his shoulders. The equalizers stood out in the puttock bockets of his acolytes. He held a little golden truncheon in his hand and there was a heavy golden grenade swinging from his belt. They went down the main staircase, and as the commissergeant's hand shot up to the rim of his helmet the sentry at the bottom leapt into the saddle of his high horse which was clearly standing on its dignity. A special car was waiting at the door. The commissergeant sat alone at the back, and the six men-at-arms spread themselves out evenly on the projecting footplates – the two fattest on one side, and the four skinny ones on the other. The driver was also wearing black leather, but had no helmet. He put his foot down. The car had no wheels, but a million tough vibrating feet of a type that ensured that there would be no risk of scattered obstacles and lost property bursting the tyres. The feet snorted and stamped on the road and the driver took a sharp turn at the first fork. The passengers felt as if they were on the surfy crest of a breaking wave.

56

As she watched Colin disappear into the distance, Alyssum's whole heart went out to him to say Good-bye. He loved Chloe so much and he was going out to look for a job because of her so that he could buy more flowers and kill the horrible monster that was eating her away inside. Colin's broad shoulders were sloping slightly. He seemed so tired. His fair hair was no longer smartly brushed and combed like it used to be.

Chick could be so charming talking about one of Heartre's books or explaining something about Heartre. It would be impossible for him to live without Heartre. It would never occur to him to think of looking for anything else – Heartre says everything for him that he would ever want to say. Heartre must be stopped from publishing that encyclopedia. It will be the death of Chick. He'll steal – even murder a bookseller. Alyssum slowly started walking. Heartre spends all day in a gin palace, drinking and writing with people like himself who also sit there writing and drinking. They drink Sea Tea and High Spirits so that they don't have to think what they're writing about. People are always going in and out, stirring up their basic ideas. Then they fish out one or two from the depths without discarding the remainder, retain a little of each, and dilute. People absorb this kind of thing much more easily, women in particular, as they can't stand anything pure. The road to the gin palace was not very long. Alyssum saw one of the waiters in a white jacket and yellow trousers serving a stuffed pig's trotter to Randy Man-O'Queue, the New Zaziland Screwball champ, whose English promotions by Rabbi Ragwrath always have such excellent posters by

H. H. Welnit-Joy. Instead of drinking, which he detested, he doted on spiced foods to give his neighbours a thirst. She went in. Jean Pulse Heartre, in his usual seat, was writing. There were lots of people and a soft buzz of voices. Through an everyday miracle – the kind that only happens on Bank Holidays – Alyssum saw an empty seat by the side of Jean Pulse and she sat down. She put her heavy bag on her knees and unzipped it. Over Jean Pulse's shoulder she could see the heading on the sheet – *Encyclopedia, Volume Nineteen*. Timidly she put a hand on Jean Pulse's arm. He stopped writing.

'Have you got that far already?' said Alyssum.

'Yes,' replied Jean Pulse. 'Do you want a word with me?'

'I've come to ask you not to publish it,' she said.

'That would be very hard,' said Jean Pulse. 'Everybody's waiting for it.'

He took off his glasses, breathed on the lenses, and put them back on again. Now his eyes could not be seen.

'Of course they are,' said Alyssum. 'I just meant that I wanted you to hold it up for a while.'

'Oh,' said Jean Pulse, 'if that's all you want, we'll see what we can do.'

'You'll have to hold it up for about ten years,' said Alyssum.

'Really?' said Jean Pulse.

'Huhum,' said Alyssum. 'Ten years at least, I'm afraid. You know it's far better to give people a chance to save up to buy it.'

'It's going to be very boring to read,' said Jean Pulse Heartre, 'because it's already terribly boring to write. I've got shocking cramp in my left wrist simply through holding the paper down.'

'You poor thing,' said Alyssum. 'I feel sorry for you.'

'Because I've got pins and needles?'

'No,' said Alyssum. 'Because you won't hold up publication.'

'Why?'

'Why? Because Chick spends all his money on buying everything you do – and he hasn't got any money left.'

'He'd be far better off buying something else,' said Jean Pulse. 'I never dream of buying any of my own books.'

'But he likes what you write.'

'He has the right to,' said Jean Pulse. 'He's made his choice.'

'I think he's too committed,' said Alyssum. 'I made a choice too, but I'm free now because he doesn't want me to live with him any more. So I'm going to kill you because you won't postpone publication.'

'But you'll take away my only means of existence,' said Jean Pulse. 'How do you think I'm going to get my royalties if I'm dead?'

'That's your funeral,' said Alyssum. 'I can't be expected to take everything into consideration since the thing I want to do more than anything is to kill you.'

'Don't you realize that I can't accept that kind of argument?' asked Jean Pulse Heartre.

'Oh, I do,' said Alyssum. She opened her bag and whipped out Chick's heart-snatcher that she'd taken from the drawer in his desk several days previously.

'Would you mind undoing your collar?' she asked.

'Listen,' said Jean Pulse, taking off his glasses, 'this whole business is idiotic.'

He unbuttoned his collar. Alyssum gathered all her strength together and, with a firm gesture, plunged the heart-snatcher into Heartre's bosom. He stared at her, died very quickly, and gave one last startled look when he saw that his heart was shaped like a tetrahedron. Alyssum turned very pale. Jean Pulse Heartre was dead now and the tea was getting cold. She took the manuscript of the *Encyclopedia* and tore it up. A waiter came and wiped up the blood and all the mess it was making mixed with the ink from Heartre's pen on the little square table-top. She tipped the waiter, released both prongs of the heart-snatcher, and Heartre's heart tumbled out on to the table. She closed up the gleaming instrument again and put it back in her bag. Then she went out into the street, holding the box of matches that she had taken from Heartre's pocket.

57

She looked round. Thick black smoke was filling the shop window and people in the street were beginning to notice. She had had to use three matches before she could get the fire started. Heartre's books were far too tough to let themselves be consumed easily. The bookseller was sprawled out under his counter. His heart, which was by his side, was beginning to burn with a black flame, and parabolic sprays of boiling blood were already spouting from it. The first two bookshops, three hundred yards behind her, were in flames, crackling, snorting, rumbling, and their owners were dead. Everyone who had sold books to Chick was going to die in the same way, and their bookshops would burn. Alyssum was running and weeping, remembering Jean Pulse Heartre's eyes when he had seen his own heart.

She hadn't meant to kill him in the first place – only to save Chick from the dreadful disaster that was slowly mounting up all round him. They were all in league against Chick – and they all wanted to rob him of his money. They preyed on his Pulse-Heartrian passion, sold him useless old rags and slobbery pipes, and they deserved everything that was coming to them. On her left she saw a window full of paperbacks. She stopped, took a deep breath, and went in. The bookseller went up to her.

'Can I help you?' he asked.

'Have you anything by Heartre?' said Alyssum.

'Of course,' said the bookseller. 'But I'm afraid I can't show you any association items at the moment. They're all reserved for a very special customer.'

'You mean Chick?' said Alyssum.

'Yes,' replied the bookseller, 'I think that's his name.'

'He won't be buying anything from you any more,' said Alyssum.

She went closer to him and dropped her handkerchief. The bookseller, bones creaking, bent down to pick it up for her and with a rapid movement she stuck the heart-snatcher in his back. She was trembling and weeping as she did it. He fell, face downwards. She did not dare pick up her handkerchief as his fingers were clenched round it. The heart-snatcher sprang back with the bookseller's heart, very small and very pink, between its prongs. She released them and the heart rolled to the side of its bookseller. She would have to hurry. She grabbed a pile of old papers, set light to them, and flung them under the counter. Then she threw more newspapers on top, piling into the flames a dozen James Bonds from the nearest shelf. The flames licked over the books, warmly, eagerly, lovingly, sadistically.

The wood of the counter smoked and cracked. Clouds of smoke filled the shop. Alyssum knocked a last shelf of books into the fire and crept out on tip-toe. She turned round the notice on the door to read *Closed* so that nobody would go in, and started running again. Her eyes were prickling and her hair smelt of smoke. She ran on and the tears had only a short journey down her cheeks now as the wind dried them straight away. She was getting close to Chick's street. There were only two or three more serious bookshops left, and the others held no danger for him. She looked round before going into the next one. Far behind her fat columns of smoke could be seen rising in the sky, with people below them hurrying to watch the complicated snakes and ladders of the Phyghre Brigade being played amongst the flames. Their big white engines shrieked past in the street as she closed the door. Her eyes followed them through the glass, and the bookseller went up to her asking if he could help her.

58

'You,' said the police commissergeant, 'stay there, on the right of the door. And you, Douglas,' he went on, turning to the second fat policeman-at-arms, 'stay on the left. And don't let anyone in.'

The two designated policemen-at-arms grabbed their equalizers, letting their right hands drop back along their right thighs, the nozzles pointing to their knees, in the regulation position. They adjusted the chinstraps of their helmets under their double chins, one of which overlapped at the front, and one at the back. The commissergeant went in, followed by the four skinny policemen-at-arms. Once again he posted one on each side of the door with orders to let nobody go out. He went up the stairs, followed by the two remaining skinny ones. They were very much alike, with sullen, scowling complexions, black eyes and thin lips.

59

Chick turned off the record-player while he changed the two records that he had just listened to simultaneously right through. As he was choosing some more from another series of lectures, he found a photo of Alyssum that he thought he had lost under one of the records. It was a three-quarter portrait in soft melting light. It seemed as if the photographer must have set up a lamp behind her to sprinkle sunshine into the silhouette of her hair. He changed the records and kept the photo in his hand. Glancing out of the window he noticed that new columns of smoke were rising, much closer now. He would listen to these two records and then go down for a chat with the bookseller next door. He sat down, held the photo with both hands before his eyes, looking at it more and more closely. It reminded him of Heartre. Little by little, Alyssum's features gave way to Heartre's, and he smiled at Chick. Of course he would dedicate anything he liked for him. Footsteps were coming up the stairs. He listened. There was a thudding, thumping and banging on the door. He put down the photo, stopped the record-player and went to see who it was. Standing there he saw the black leather uniform of one of the policemen-at-arms, then the second and, last but by no means least, the commissergeant in red. Fleeting reflections from the twilight of the landing were slithering over his black helmet.

'Is your name Chick?' said the commissergeant.

Chick stepped back and his face went pale. He went back as far as the wall where his precious books were arranged.

'What am I supposed to have done?' he asked.

The commissergeant fumbled in his breast pocket and read his warrant. 'Collection of overdue taxes from Chick Esquire, following seizure of coinage. Smuggling contraband tobacco with serious indictment. Total, or at least partial, confiscation of goods, aggravated by breaking up of happy home.'

'But . . . I promise you I'll pay my income tax,' said Chick.

'Oh, yes,' said the commissergeant. 'But not until we've done with you . . . First of all we must charge you with contraband tobacco. It's a very strong kind of smoke – we use the shortened title so that people don't get alarmed about it.'

'I'll give you all my money,' said Chick.

'Of course,' said the commissergeant.

Chick went to his desk and opened the drawer. He kept a very powerful heart-snatcher in there, and a rather rusty rozza-eraser. He couldn't find the heart-snatcher, but he could feel the rozza-eraser under a pile of papers.

'I hope it's the money you're looking for in there,' said the commissergeant.

The two policemen-at-arms had spread out, each holding his equalizer. Chick sprang round with his rozza-eraser in his hand.

'Look out, chief!' said one of the policemen-at-arms.

'Shall I squeeze the trigger, chief?' asked the second.

'You won't get me like that,' said Chick . . .

'All right,' said the commissergeant, 'if that's the way you want to play it, we'll take your books.'

One of the policemen-at-arms grabbed the first book that he could reach. He opened it roughly and its spine cracked.

'Nothing in it but words, chief,' he proclaimed.

'Pulp it!' said the commissergeant.

The policeman-at-arms seized the book by its binding and shook it viciously. Chick screamed.

'Don't touch it . . . Leave it alone!'

'Now, now,' said the commissergeant. 'Why don't you use your rozza-eraser then? You know very well that my warrant says *Breaking up of the happy home*!'

'Put it down,' Chick roared again, raising his rozza-eraser. But it was old and worn-out, and crumbled in his hands.

'Shall I pull my trigger, chief?' asked the policeman-at-arms again.

The book fell from its binding and Chick rushed forward, dropping the useless rozza-eraser.

'Shoot, Douglas!' said the commissergeant, stepping back.

Chick's body sank to the floor between the feet of the policemen-at-arms. They had both fired at once.

'Shall we pass the contraband tobacco now, chief?' asked the other policeman-at-arms.

Chick was still moving a little. He raised himself up on his hands and managed to kneel. He was clutching his stomach and his face twitched dreadfully as drops of sweat fell into his eyes. There was a great gash in his forehead.

'Don't touch my books . . .' he burbled. His voice was thick and indistinct.

'We're going to pulp them with our boots,' said the commissergeant. 'In a few seconds you'll be dead.'

Chick's head fell back. He made a gigantic effort to raise it again, but his stomach hurt as if triangular blades were churning over inside it. He managed to put one foot on the ground, but the other knee refused to bend. The policemen-at-arms closed in on the books while the commissergeant took two steps nearer to Chick.

'Leave those books alone . . .' gasped Chick. The gurgling blood made a horrible noise in his throat, and his head lurched over even more grotesquely. He let go of his stomach and his scarlet hands aimlessly beat the air. He fell down again, his face hitting the floor. The commissergeant turned him over with his foot. He did not move any more and his open eyes focused on something far beyond the confines of his room. His face was completely cut in half by the streak of blood which had trickled down from his forehead.

'Give it to him, Douglas!' said the commissergeant. 'I'll smash up the din-grinder personally.'

He went to the window and saw that a fat mushroom of smoke was slowly bellowing up towards him from the ground floor of the house next door.

'Don't bother to be too careful,' he added. 'The house next door is on fire. Be quick – that's all! There'll be no traces left of anything – but I'll write it all up beautifully in my report.'

Chick's face was completely blackened. The pool of blood beneath his body was slowly coagulating into a star.

60

Nicholas walked past the last bookshop but one which Alyssum had set on fire. He had seen Colin going off to his work and heard how upset his niece was. He had heard about Heartre's death as soon as he had rung his club, and had set off to find Alyssum. He wanted to console her and cheer her up and ask her to stay with him until she became her old happy self again. He saw Chick's house. A long thin tongue of flame spat out of the middle of the window of the bookshop next door and split the glass like a hammer-blow. In front of the door he noticed the commissergeant's car and saw that the driver was moving it on a little to get out of the danger-zone. He noticed the black silhouettes of the policemen-at-arms too. The Phyghre-phyghters came along almost immediately. Their engine stopped outside the bookshop with a fearful screech. Nicholas was already struggling with the *Closed* sign. He managed to kick down the door and rushed inside. The whole of the back of the shop was ablaze. The bookseller's body was stretched out – his feet in the flames, his heart by his side – and he saw Chick's heart-snatcher lying on the floor. Great balls of red fire lashed out at him and with forked tongues which pierced the thick walls of the shop with a single lick. Nicholas flung himself down on the ground so that he wouldn't be burnt and, as he did so, he felt a violent rush of air above him caused by the extinguishing spray from the Phyghre Brigade's equipment. The noise of the fire doubled as the horizontal fountain attacked it from the base. Books were burning and crackling, and flapping pages flew up far above Nicholas's head, away from the spray. He could hardly breathe in all the din and the flames. He thought that Alyssum would hardly have stayed in the fire, but he couldn't see any door she might have escaped by. The fire was struggling against the Phyghremen and seemed to be rapidly rising, breaking loose from the lower zone which was beginning to die out. In the midst of the dull grey cinders there still remained one brilliant glowing patch, more vivid than all the flames.

The smoke drifted away very quickly, sucked up towards the floors above. The books were going out, but the ceiling was burning more fiercely than ever. Nothing was left on the ground but that pure brilliant glow.

His hair blackened, covered with ashes, hardly able to breathe, Nicholas plunged ahead, fighting to reach the light. He could hear the boots of the Phyghre-phyghters trampling above. Under a girder of twisted steel he caught a glimpse of a blindingly blonde fleece. The flames had been unable to devour it, for it shone more brilliantly than they could. He put it in his inside pocket and went out.

He walked with an unsure step. The Phyghre-phyghters watched him go. The fire was still raging on the floors above and they were getting ready to isolate the block and let it burn itself out as there was no extinguishing liquid left.

61

Colin could just see the thirtieth pillar. All morning he had been walking round and round the cellar of the Gold Reserve. His job was to yell when he saw anybody coming to steal the gold. The vaults were enormous. It took a whole day, going very quickly, to go completely round them. In the centre was the strong-room where the gold was slowly maturing in a mixture of lethal gases. This job was extremely well-paid, providing you could manage to get all the way round in a day. Colin didn't feel that he was physically fit enough, and the vaults were too dark for him. He found himself looking back from time to time and getting behind on his time-table. He could see nothing behind him but the tiny gleaming speck of the last lamp, and nothing ahead of him but the next lamp which slowly grew larger.

The gold thieves did not come every day, but the check-points had to be visited at the scheduled time all the same, otherwise a fine would be deducted from his wages. The time-table had to be adhered to so that he could be ready to shout when the robbers arrived. They were men with very regular habits.

Colin's right foot hurt. The vaults, constructed of hard artificial stone, had a rough, uneven floor. He forced himself to go on. He stumbled a little when going over the eighth white line, trying to reach the thirtieth pillar on time. He started singing as he walked, but soon refrained from his refrain because the echo made menacing mince-meat of his words and put them to all the wrong tunes.

With his legs aching, he went on unrelentingly, and passed the thirtieth pillar. He looked round automatically thinking he could see something behind him. He lost another five seconds and ran a few steps in order to catch up with himself.

62

It was no longer possible to get into the dining-room. The ceiling was almost touching the floor and half-vegetable, half-mineral projections reached out to clasp each other across the dark humidity. The corridor door would not open. All that was left was a narrow space leading to Chloe's bedroom from the entrance. Isis went in first, and Nicholas followed her. He seemed stunned. Something bulged inside his jacket and from time to time he put his hand on his chest.

Isis looked at the bed before she went into the room. Chloe was still surrounded by flowers. Her hands, stretched out on the blankets, were hardly able to hold the big white orchid that was in them. It looked grey by the side of her diaphanous skin. Her eyes were open but she hardly moved when she saw Isis come and sit down by her side. When Nicholas saw Chloe he looked away again. He wanted to smile at her, but he simply went up and touched her hand. He too sat down and Chloe gently closed her eyes, then opened them again. She seemed happy to see them.

'Were you asleep?' Isis whispered.

Chloe's eyes said *No*. Her thin fingers reached for Isis's hand. Under her other hand she was hiding the mouse whose sparkling black eyes gleamed out at them. It trotted across the bed to sit near Nicholas. He picked it up gently, kissing its glossy little nose, and then it went back to Chloe. The flowers round the bed trembled. They did not last very long, and Chloe could feel herself growing weaker every hour.

'Where's Colin?' asked Isis.

'Work . . .' breathed Chloe.

'Don't try to talk,' said Isis. 'I'll talk so that you won't have to speak.'

She put her pretty dark head close to Chloe's and kissed her tenderly.

'Is he working at the bank?' she said.

Chloe's eyelids closed.

They heard a footstep in the hall. Colin appeared at the door. He was holding some fresh flowers, but he had lost his job. The robbers had gone through too quickly and he could hardly walk any more. As he had been doing his best he had earned a little money – these flowers.

Chloe seemed calmer. She almost managed a smile now, and Colin went as close to her as he could. He loved her too much for the strength she had, and he hardly touched her now for fear of breaking her to pieces. With his aching hand, still bearing the scars of work, he stroked her dark hair.

Nicholas, Colin, Isis and Chloe were there. A slow tear rolled down Nicholas's cheek because Chick and Alyssum would never be there again, and because Chloe was so ill.

63

The management gave Colin plenty of money – but it was too late. Every day he had to go and see people. They gave him a list and he had to bring bad tidings a day before they were going to happen.

Every day he went out into the crowded streets or into society. He went up and down thousands of stairs. Nobody was pleased to see him. They threw pots and pans at his head, drove fierce harsh words through his ears, and then kicked him out of their doors. He got well paid for this and pleased the management. For once he kept his job. It was the only thing he could do well – get himself kicked out.

He was harrowed by fatigue which stiffened his knees and hollowed his cheeks. His eyes saw only the ugliness of people. He went on telling them the terrible things that were going to happen. He went on being chased away by sticks, stones, blood, tears and curses.

He went up the steps, along the corridor and knocked, taking another step back almost immediately. People knew as soon as they saw his big black helmet so they treated him badly, but Colin couldn't complain as he was being paid to do it. The door opened. He said his piece and went away. A heavy block of wood hit him in the back of the neck.

He looked at the next name on the list and saw that it was his own. Then he threw down his helmet and he walked slowly home with his heart as heavy as lead for he knew that by tomorrow Chloe would be dead.

64

Father Phigga was deep in conversation with the Husher, and Colin waited until they had finished talking before he went up to them. He could no longer see the ground beneath his feet and he kept tripping over. His eyes saw Chloe, pale on their honeymoon bed, with her dark hair and her tiny nose, her smooth forehead, her sweet round face and her eyelids which, when they had closed, had separated the world from her.

'Have you come about a funeral?' said Father Phigga.

'Chloe's dead,' said Colin.

He heard Colin say 'Chloe's dead', but thought he must have been mistaken.

'I know,' said Father Phigga. 'How much do you want to spend? You'd like one of our loveliest services, of course?'

'Yes,' said Colin.

'I can do you something very nice for about two thousand doublezoons,' said Father Phigga. 'For a trifle more . . .'

'I've only got twenty doublezoons,' said Colin. 'I might be able to get thirty or forty more, but not straight away.'

Father Phigga filled his lungs and emptied them with an air of disgust.

'Then all you can afford is a pauper's funeral.'

'I am a pauper . . .' said Colin. 'And Chloe is dead . . .'

'Yes, yes,' said Father Phigga. 'But you should always try to see to it that you die with enough money to get yourself decently buried. Haven't you even got five hundred doublezoons?'

'No,' said Colin . . . 'I might be able to raise a hundred if I could pay a little each week. Do you realize what it means to have to say to yourself that "Chloe is dead"? . . .'

'Oh,' said Father Phigga, 'I'm used to it, so it doesn't have any effect on me any more. I ought to advise you to address yourself to God, but I'm afraid that for such a small sum it isn't worth interrupting him . . .'

'Don't worry,' said Colin. 'I won't disturb him. I don't think he'd be able to do much anyway, you see, because Chloe is dead . . .'

'Let's change the subject,' said Father Phigga. 'Think of . . . Oh, I don't know . . . Think of something else . . . Such as . . .'

'Can I have a decent service for a hundred double-zoons?' said Colin.

'I don't even want to envisage that solution,' said Father Phigga. 'You'll have to go to a hundred and fifty.'

'It'll take me some time to pay you.'

'You're working, aren't you? . . . You just have to sign a little piece of paper . . .'

'All right . . .' said Colin.

'In that case,' said Father Phigga, 'maybe you could go up to two hundred, and then you'll have the Unisexton Bedull and the Husher on your side. For a hundred and fifty they're still on the opposition.'

'I don't think I can manage that,' said Colin. 'I don't think I'll be able to keep my job much longer.'

'Well, then, we'll say a hundred and fifty,' concluded Father Phigga. 'It's a pity, because it really will be lousy. You tight-fisted people make me sick, trying to cut everything down all the time . . .'

'I'm sorry,' said Colin.

'Come and sign the forms,' said Father Phigga, giving him a brutal shove.

Colin fell against a chair. Father Phigga, infuriated by the noise, pushed him once more towards the sacristicks and grousingly followed him.

65

The two porters found Colin waiting for them at the entrance to the flat. They were covered in grime because the staircase had almost completely disintegrated. But they had their oldest clothes on, and there wasn't much room left for any more patches in them. Through the holes in their uniforms you could see the ginger hair on their thongy legs. They greeted Colin with a punch in the stomach – as is laid down in the rules for a pauper's funeral.

The entrance was now more like the inside of a cave. They had to lower their heads to get into Chloe's bedroom. The coffin-men had already gone. There were no signs of Chloe, but just an old battered black box, marked with the order number. They grabbed hold of it and, using it as a battering-ram, shot it through the window. Corpses were only carried down by hand from five hundred double-zoons upwards.

'No wonder the box is so bashed about,' thought Colin, and he wept because Chloe must have been bruised and broken inside it.

He dreamt that she could no longer feel anything – and this made him weep even more. The box landed on the cobbles with a clatter and broke the leg of a child playing in the gutter. They pushed it on to the pavement and lifted it on to the funeral cart. It was an old lorry painted red and one of the two porters drove it.

Very few people followed the lorry. Just Nicholas, Isis and Colin, and two or three people that they did not even know. The lorry went fairly fast and they had to run to keep up with it. The driver was singing out loud. He only shut up from over two hundred and fifty doublezoons.

They stopped in front of the church and the black box was left outside while they went in for the service. Father Phigga, sullen and surly, turned his back on them and began moving about meaninglessly. Colin was left standing before the altar.

He raised his eyes and saw Jesus hanging on his cross above the altar-rail in front of him. He looked fed up and Colin said to him, 'Why did Chloe have to die?'

'Nothing to do with me,' said Jesus. 'It's not my responsibility. Let's talk about something else . . .'

'Whose responsibility is it then?' asked Colin.

They were talking together quietly and the others could not hear what they were saying.

'Not mine, at any rate,' said Jesus.

'I *did* ask you to my wedding,' said Colin.

'That was fun,' said Jesus. 'I had a smashing time. Why don't you spend a bit more money now?'

'There's none left,' said Colin. 'And anyway, this isn't a wedding . . .'

'Um,' said Jesus.

He looked as if he felt awkward.

'This is something very different,' said Colin. 'This time, Chloe's dead . . . I can't bear to think about that black box.'

'Mmmmmm . . .' said Jesus.

He looked somewhere else and seemed bored again. Father Phigga swung a rattle while shouting a Latin chorus.

'Why did you make her die?' asked Colin.

'Oh! . . .' said Jesus. 'Shut up.'

He wriggled to get more comfortable on his nails.

'She was so sweet,' said Colin. 'She never did anything bad – and she never had an evil thought.'

'That's nothing to do with religion,' mumbled Jesus with a yawn.

He shook his head to the other side to change the angle of his crown of thorns.

'I don't know what we did to deserve this,' said Colin.

He lowered his eyes. Jesus did not reply. Colin raised

his head. Jesus's chest was going gently up and down. His features were smooth and calm. His eyes were closed and Colin could hear a soft smug purring sound coming from his nostrils like an overfed cat. At this moment Father Phigga jumped from one foot to the other, blew down a tube, and the service was over.

Father Phigga was first to leave the church and went back into the sacristicks to put on his big hob-nailed boots.

Colin, Isis and Nicholas went out and waited behind the lorry.

Then the Husher and Adam Browbeadle, the Unisexton Bedull, appeared, richly dressed in their brightest colours. They began to hoot at Colin and danced round the lorry like savages. Colin stuffed his ears, but he said nothing as he had agreed to a pauper's burial. He did not even flinch when their fistfuls of stones began to hit him.

66

They walked through the streets for a very long time. People had stopped looking round and the daylight was fading. The pauper's graveyard was quite a long way away. The red lorry rolled along, jumping over the bumps in the road while the motor let out joyful bangs and explosions.

Colin heard nothing. He was living in the past and occasionally smiled as he remembered it all. Nicholas and Isis were walking behind him. Now and again Isis would touch Colin's shoulder.

The road stopped – and the lorry too. They had reached the water's edge. The porters dragged down the black box.

It was the first time Colin had been to the cemetery. It was hidden away on a nebulous island whose shore-line was constantly changing with the shifting tides. It could be seen only vaguely through the drifting fog. The lorry was left on the shore. The island was reached by a long springy plank whose furthermost extremity disappeared into the mist. The porters let out five great funereal oaths and one of them ventured on to the plank. It was just wide enough to be walked on. They put thick ropes over their shoulders and round their necks to carry the black box. The second porter was nearly suffocated and turned purple. It looked very sad against the grey of the fog. Colin followed. In turn, Nicholas and Isis set out along the plank. The first porter deliberately jumped on it to make it wobble and swing to right and left. He disappeared in the midst of a cloud which drifted across like strands of sugar in a syrupy solution. Their steps echoed along the plank in a descending scale. It curved more and more as they drew nearer to the centre. When they were there, the plank touched the water and symmetrical wavelets went out on each side. The water almost covered it. It was dark, but looked transparent. Colin leaned over to the right, thinking he could see something white vaguely moving in the depths below. Nicholas and Isis stopped behind him. They seemed to be standing on the water. The porters trudged on. The second half of the journey was uphill and when they had gone past the middle the little waves grew smaller and the plank detached itself from the water with a little sucking noise.

The porters began to run. As they stamped their feet the handles of the black box rattled against its sides. They reached the island before Colin and his friends and plodded heavily up the little winding path between thick hedges of dark sinister plants. The path wriggled, turned and twisted in peculiar ways past desolate landmarks. Then it became dry and crumbly and began to widen out a little. The leaves of the plants were a lighter grey, and their veins stood out in a silver filigree on their velvet flesh. The trees, long and supple, curved in an arc from one side of the road to the other. The daylight made a dull white glow through the vault formed between them. The path branched off into several different directions – but the porters automatically turned to the right. Colin, Isis and Nicholas had to run to keep up with them. No signs of life were heard in the trees, but occasionally a grey leaf would fall flatly to the earth. They followed all the twists and turns of the road. The porters kicked the tree trunks and their heavy boots left deep purple bruises in the spongy bark. The cemetery was right in the middle of the island. By scrambling on to rocks the other shore could be seen far away, over the tops of the sparse straggling trees. The sky there was scratched with fierce graffiti by two-headed eaglets flying low over fields of chick-weed and fennel.

The porters stopped near a big hole. They began to swing Chloe's coffin, singing 'Roll Me Over'. Then they pressed the catch. The lid opened and something fell into the hole with a deep thud. The second porter went down flat, half strangled because the rope round his neck had not been loosened quickly enough. Colin and Nicholas came along, running, with Isis stumbling behind them. Then Adam Browbeadle and the Husher, in old oily rags, suddenly sprang out from behind a tuffet, yelling and howling like wolves and flinging stones and earth into the hole.

Colin had sunk down on to his knees with his head in his

hands. The stones made a dull sound as they went down. The Husher, Adam Browbeadle and the two porters held hands, danced in a ring round the hole, and then dashed off down the path as fast as their little legs would carry them, playing 'Follow My Leader', until they disappeared over the horizon. Adam Browbeadle blew into a double-clarionet and the brittle sounds rang out through the still air. The earth began to crumble and tumble in little by little and, after a very short time, Chloe's body had completely disappeared.

67

The grey mouse with the black whiskers made one final effort and at last got through. Behind it the ceiling sharply crashed down to the floor and long worms of grey spaghetti oozed out, slowly twisting through the cracks and broken joints. The mouse scooted as fast as it could across the darkened corridor whose trembling walls were crumbling closer and closer together, and managed to squeeze under the door. It reached the staircase and tumbled down, head over heels. Only when it was on the pavement did it stop. It stood still for a second, thought about which way to go, and started off again for the boneyard.

68

'To tell the truth,' said the cat, 'I don't really find the proposition very exciting.'

'But you're so wrong,' said the mouse. 'I'm still quite young and, until quite recently, I was very well fed.'

'But I'm well fed now,' said the cat, 'and I haven't got the slightest desire to commit suicide. That's why I find it all so extraordinary.'

'But then *you* didn't know him,' said the little mouse.

'Tell me about him,' said the cat.

It didn't really want to know. It was a warm day and the tips of its fur were tingling.

'He's standing at the water's edge,' said the mouse, 'waiting. When it's visiting time, he steps on to the plank and waits in the middle. He can see something.'

'I shouldn't think he could see much,' said the cat. 'Perhaps it's a water-lily.'

'Probably,' said the mouse. 'He's waiting for it to come up so that he can kill it.'

'That's stupid,' said the cat. 'It's not in the least bit inspiring.'

'When visiting time is over,' the mouse went on, 'he goes back on the bank and stares at her photo.'

'Doesn't he ever eat anything?' asked the cat.

'No,' said the mouse, 'and he's growing so weak. I can't bear it. One of these days he's going to slip.'

'Why should you care?' asked the cat. 'Is he unhappy?'

'He's not unhappy,' said the mouse, 'He's grieving. And that's what I can't bear. One day he'll fall into the water through leaning over too far.'

'Well,' said the cat, 'if that's the way it is, I'll see what I can do for you – although I don't know why I said "If that's the way it is", because I really don't understand what all the fuss is about.'

'It's very kind of you,' said the mouse.

'Just put your head in my mouth,' said the cat, 'and wait.'

'Will it take long?' asked the mouse.

'Only until somebody treads on my tail,' said the cat. 'I just need something to make me jump. I'll leave it stretched out, so don't worry.'

The mouse opened the cat's jaws and placed its head between the sharp teeth. It pulled it out again almost as quickly.

'Ugh!' it said. 'Did you have shark for breakfast?'

'Now look here,' said the cat, 'if you don't like it, you can clear off. The whole story's a bore. You'll have to manage by yourself.'

It seemed angry.

'Don't lose your temper,' said the mouse.

It closed its little black eyes and put its head back. The cat let its pointed canine teeth close delicately on the soft grey throat. The mouse's black whiskers brushed against the cat's. The cat's bushy tail unrolled across the pavement.

The voices of eleven little girls, coming in a crocodile from the Orphanage of Pope John the Twenty-third, could be heard getting nearer. They were singing. And they were blind.

Memphis, 8 March 1946
Davenport, 10 March 1946

Anglicized
Carnaby Street, 28 December 1966
King's Road, 21 February 1967